Renegade Boys 2

Meesha

Lock Down Publications and Ca$h
Presents
Renegade Boys 2
A Novel by *Meesha*

Meesha

Lock Down Publications
P.O. Box 870494
Mesquite, Tx 75187

Visit our website @
www.lockdownpublications.com

Copyright 2019 Renegade Boys 2

First Edition February 2019
Printed in the United States of America

This is a work of fiction. Names, characters, places, and incidents either are products of the author's imagination or are used ficti-tiously. Any similarity to actual events or locales or persons, living or dead, is entirely coincidental.

Lock Down Publications
Like our page on Facebook: Lock Down Publications @
www.facebook.com/lockdownpublications.ldp
Cover design and layout by: **Dynasty Cover Me**
Book interior design by: **Shawn Walker**
Edited by: **Tam Jernigan**

Stay Connected with Us!

Text **LOCKDOWN** to 22828 to stay up-to-date with new releases, sneak peaks, contests and more…
Or **CLICK HERE** to sign up.
Thank you.

Like our page on Facebook:

Lock Down Publications: Facebook

Join Lock Down Publications/The New Era Reading Group

Visit our website @
www.lockdownpublications.com

Follow us on Instagram:

Lock Down Publications: Instagram

Email Us: We want to hear from you!

Submission Guideline.

Submit the first three chapters of your completed manuscript to ldpsubmissions@gmail.com, subject line: Your book's title. The manuscript must be in a .doc file and sent as an attachment. Document should be in Times New Roman, double spaced and in size 12 font. Also, provide your synopsis and full contact information. If sending multiple submissions, they must each be in a separate email.

Have a story but no way to send it electronically? You can still submit to LDP/Ca$h Presents. Send in the first three chapters, written or typed, of your completed manuscript to:

LDP: Submissions Dept
Po Box 870494
Mesquite, Tx 75187

DO NOT send original manuscript. Must be a duplicate.

Provide your synopsis and a cover letter containing your full contact information.

Thanks for considering LDP and Ca$h Presents.

Author's Note

I want to thank every one of my readers that has rocked with me from the start. This has been a surreal experience for me. Book 7! I still can't believe that I've been able to continue wowing ya'll! I can't thank you guys enough for motivating me to push harder with every book that I've released. Without y'all, there wouldn't be an Author Meesha. Thank you, thank you, thank you from the bottom of my heart. Renegade Boys is my best work to date and I put my all into it and I owe it to all of you. So, this book is dedicated to everyone that has shown me love, and support. Meesha

Meesha

Chapter 1
Sosa

The realization of what happened hit me. My brother was gone. After I broke down in the parking lot of the hospital, it took about a half hour for me to calm down. My heart was torn in a million pieces. I felt like everything was my fault because papí gave me a warning before I even left the house that night to keep an eye on Max. I failed at the one task I was given and there was no way for me to correct it.

Mauricio was by my side and I was feeding off the little bit of energy that resonated from him. "Come on, brah. We need to go inside and sign these papers so we can get the arrangements going for Max. The funeral home won't be able to pick him up if it's not done."

"Them muthafuckas killed him, Ricio! They got to pay for this shit! Not only did they have papí killed, they got mama and Max too. We can't sit around waiting for them to add us to their body count. We have to hit them first. On my family, there's gonna be a bloody massacre in this city. I'm ready to do a life sentence as long as I get justice for them."

"No doubt, I'll be standing right next to you when the shit goes down. We all we got and if that means we going to prison together, so be it. That shit gotta wait though because we have to go back inside and handle things with Max. Stop procrastinating, Sosa." Ricio said pulling me in for a brotherly hug. "We gon' be straight, my nigga. We gon' be straight."

Taking a deep breath, I was struggling because I felt like I was about to start hyperventilating. Seeing Max in that state was something I wasn't prepared for. I'd seen plenty of dead bodies and many were by my own hands, but none of them was my brother. This was something totally different.

Ricio led me to the entrance and my feet felt like cement blocks were attached to them. The entire team was behind us as we approached the front desk. Nija stood up from the chair she was sitting in and fell in line next to Ricio and grabbed his left hand.

"We're ready to go back to see Maximo Vasquez." Ricio said in a shaky voice.

The nurse that he snapped on earlier was sitting behind the desk. Her entire attitude was different from the one she'd presented earlier. "We usually don't let this many people in at once, but the doctor is making an exception. I'll be leading you all into the room personally. Sorry for your loss." She stated as she came around the counter.

Walking down the hall seemed to take forever when it was only a few minutes. No one said anything as we made our way to the room. As we got closer to Max, I could smell the copper scent of blood in the air and my stomach churned. Ricio and Nija were the first to enter. My feet stopped automatically and Beast ran into my back.

"You good, nephew?" he asked placing his hand on my shoulder.

"Yeah, go on in. I'm gon' wait out here for a few minutes." Nija's cries erupted through the halls and I stumbled back against the wall and slid to the floor.

"Oh Max! It wasn't your time to go! You had so much more life to live!" she sobbed. "Wake up, Max. Please wake up!"

Her cries hit me in my chest like a ton of bricks and all I could do was cover my ears with my hands. Nija was truly the sister Max and I never had. She'd been there with us through all the shit that went down throughout the years.

Hearing her cry let me know that she was hurting just as much as we were.

"Nija baby, he's gone. He will never wake up again." I heard Ricio say to her. "Come on, let's go outside so you can get some air."

"I got her, Ricio." Sin said leading Nija out of the room.

The pain that was etched on Nija's face was something I'd remember for a long time. Each person that exited the room had a somber look on their face. Ricio and Beast were the only two left in the room. I still hadn't moved from the spot I was sitting in on the floor. I couldn't get up to go in the room no matter how hard I tried. The guilt was eating me alive but at the same time, I felt myself changing into something I didn't recognize.

"Sosa, they want to take him down to the morgue until the funeral home comes to collect his body. Ricio signed the paperwork already so you don't have to worry about any of that. Get up so you can see him beforehand." Beast said holding out his hand to help me up.

Accepting his hand, he pulled me from the floor and I walked slowly toward the room. Max was laying on the bed with the sheet pulled up to his neck. He looked like he was sleeping except for the fact that he hated sleeping on his back. The light snores that usually escaped his nose while he slept weren't heard, and his chest wasn't rising at all.

"I can't go in there." I said rushing down the hall to the waiting room.

"Sosa!" Beast bellowed.

I ignored him and kept going until I made it out the door. The tears were streaming down my face and I couldn't stop them from falling. Seeing Max lying there confirmed what I wasn't trying to believe. I wouldn't be able to hear him bitching about everything anymore. He wouldn't be coming to my house at three in the morning rummaging through my refrigerator because he was high. My phone wasn't going to ring with him on the other end telling me to come to Madysen's house before he kicked her ass.

"This shit is all my fault!" I yelled out loud.

"Sosa! This is not your fault." Beast said coming up behind me.

"Yes, it is! I got a warning to keep an eye on him and I didn't do that! He shouldn't have been able to get out of that door, Beast."

"Let me tell you something. From where I was, Max knew exactly what he was doing. The whole crew had tools in their hands rushing for that door. Max was the only one running blindly and empty handed. I tried to get to him before he made it to the door but I was too late. Whatever the hell was on his mind, he wanted to end shit, Sosa. I hate to say this but, that shit looked like a suicide mission."

What Beast said stopped me from pacing and my mind went back to the club when I was talking to Max. He had been drinking nonstop without a care in the world. His nonchalant attitude was what had me sitting close to him throughout the party.

"Brah, I think you should grab something to eat before you drink anything else."

"I'm not hungry," he said throwing another shot back.

"Floyd and his crew's here. I need you to stop drinking because shit is about to get real, brah. You strapped right?"

"Nah, I didn't bring it inside with me. It's in my ride." *He responded.*

I tried to give him the .25 that I had attached to my ankle but he refused it, which was unusual.

12

"Here, take this."

"Sosa, I'm not worried about shit, I'm here to have fun. There's too many muthafuckas in here for them to start a gunfight in this club. We cool, calm down."

Remembering when I told him that Floyd and his crew was inside the club, he downed a couple shots before he got to his feet. Max prepared himself with liquid courage to battle Floyd without a weapon.

"What the fuck happened when he went to the prison?" I asked softly.

"I don't know, but I'm gon' find out. That nigga Big Jim had him spooked. The truth will be revealed and all of them will pay." Beast said.

The automatic doors to the hospital opened and Ricio led the pack out with Nija by his side. Sin walked straight to Beast and fell in his arms. When she lifted her head, her hazel eyes were coal black and rimmed red. I knew at that moment that she was no longer Sincere, she was in full blown Sin City mode.

"Who's willing to take me to my car? I'm ready to go home and lay down." I didn't speak to anyone in particular.

"You know I got you, brah." Ricio said.

"Did anyone check on Madysen?" I asked looking around.

"I went in and checked on her." Sin spoke up. "She has to stay for observation because she is still in shock and they are worried about her state of mind. I left my contact information so they can call me before she is released. I'll come pick her up myself." she stated.

"Thank you, Sin." I said. She nodded her head and walked to Beast's car to wait for him.

Looking around at the crew, it was going to be hard not seeing Max and Butta amongst us. My eyes landed on Ricio and he was handing Nija his keys to go to the car. That meant he wanted to talk to us without the ladies. Once Nija was safely in the car, Ricio turned back to us.

"I want everybody to meet me at my house tomorrow at noon. It's time to get shit in order, ain't no waiting."

"Nah, we will meet at 136th and Halsted. We're an organization now, so we will conduct ourselves in that manner." Beast said.

"What type of spot is that?" I asked.

"It's a warehouse Reese purchased years ago. Now it belongs to y'all. That is where all meetings will be held, and that's where we will be storing all product. You are correct, Ricio. It's time to regulate shit and takeover this muthafuckin' city."

"Noon. Not a minute later. I'll see y'all then." Ricio said walking to his car. "Sosa are you coming?"

"Yeah, give me a minute." I shouted back at his back. "Psycho!" I yelled out to him before he could get to his ride. He stopped and his shoulders drooped. I jogged over to where he was and stopped in front of him. The hurt was written on his face and I felt bad about how I treated him. "Look, fam. I'm sorry for coming at you the way I did. If I blame you for what happened to Max, I may as well blame myself too. Nothing could've prevented him from going out of that door. This effects all of us and I needed to apologize to you."

"Sosa, it's all good. I have to go sit back and blow something because this shit is weighing heavy on my mental. One minute we were having a good time, then all hell broke loose the next. He was just a kid, man! He had his whole life ahead of him. There's no turning back from this. They killed my brother and I swear, every one of them muthafuckas are gon' feel this heat. I don't give a fuck who wasn't there, all them niggas getting it!" He said as a lone tear cascaded down his face. "I'm outta here, brah. Watch ya back because we don't know what the fuck these cowards got up their sleeves."

We dapped up and I watched him get in his whip and peeled off. I walked slowly to Ricio's car and Beast pulled up beside me. Turning my head to look at the hospital, I still felt Max's presence and didn't want to leave.

"Nephew, go get in the car. We will discuss everything tomorrow. Max is good, he is in a better place than we'll ever be. I know shit's hard for you right now but we are about to be on top of this. When I say we, it's us over everything," Beast said.

"Get ready to make them thangs clap, Sosa. I'm going home to get my shit ready. Retirement is history for this gutta bitch. Sin City is out and about, they killed the wrong muthafucka tonight. A woman is a deadly bitch to have on the team. I'm gunning for all them hoe ass niggas. Rest up because we ain't waiting too long, tomorrow is day one of operation get back." Sin said letting her head hit the headrest closing her eyes.

"Sin you ain't coming to the warehouse!" Beast spoke softly to her.

"Shid, you got me fucked up. Ain't shit gon' stop me from strappin' up to get in on this. Get ready to turn back the hands of time because they just brought the devil outta hidin'. So, you can save all that bullshit you talking right now. You know how the fuck we got down back in the day. Ain't shit changed but the date on the calendar. There won't be no talking me out of it. I'm all the way in and there's nothing else to discuss."

Sin said that shit without opening her eyes. I knew she meant business at that moment. Beast did too because he had nothing to say in return. The only thing he could do was stare at the side of her face and shake his head.

"Let me get her ass home. I'll see you tomorrow. We got to go check out the storage locker too. There's a lot that we have to get underway, but this city is about to be ours," he said dapping me up.

"Fa sho, Unc. Be easy and I'll holla at ya later. Drive carefully and keep ya eyes open."

"My shit is always open except when I'm eating pussy. Goodnight nephew," he said driving off.

Ricio pulled up and I hopped in the back seat. My eyes instantly closed but popped open again when the image of my little brother laying on that bed entered my mind. I knew this would be one night that I wouldn't get a wink of sleep.

Chapter 2
Floyd

When I found out that them niggas was gon' be at Paradise Kitty, I knew me and my crew had to show up. Big Jim called and told me that Max lil soft ass was trying to throw around ultimatums, I was only gonna catch his ass and slap him up. He wasn't the one I wanted to fall to this gun shit, one of his bitch ass brothers were the ones I was gunning for. I didn't know who got hit until I saw him drop to the ground and his bitch ran to him screaming.

I actually let a tear drop for his ass because he didn't deserve that shit. The way he came running out, it seemed like the nigga knew what was gon' happen. One thing I could say was, his secret died with him, so I was cool with the outcome. Wishing death on someone ain't my thang but I was glad his ass couldn't talk. That's one thing I didn't need spreading through the hood. What I do inside the comfort of my home was nobody's business.

My mind flashed back to when I hit Max up to come to the crib. He had always been a materialistic nigga and I knew he was eager to get his belongings before I threw them away. Telling him he had an hour to get there, put pep in his step.

Max came to the house the day before to pick up his shit. When he entered the crib, I was sitting in my La-Z Boy snorting that white girl. The shit made my dick harder than a muthafucka and I was ready to fuck his ass something serious.

"What's up Max?" I asked wiping the cocaine from my nose.

"Don't say shit to me, Floyd. Keep putting that shit up ya nose, I'm here to get my shit and I will be outta ya way."

"You think it's that easy, huh?" I asked standing up.

He walked past me and went into the bedroom that he used to sleep in. Following behind him, I caught him bending over into the closet. Gathering all of his shoes and stuffing them in a duffle bag. His ass looked real good with his pants sitting under his cheeks. I'd never touched him before but I heard the way he squealed with Big Jim and I wanted in.

Easing up behind him, I rubbed his ass and he shot up like a jack in the box. The way he stared at me almost made me laugh. He was trying to act all hard and shit but I knew the real. That shocked shit wasn't gon' work with me.

"I want you, Max. You gon' let me hit or nah?" I asked in a low tone.

"Hell nawl, nigga. Gon' somewhere with that bullshit!"

"It's either you gon' give it to me, or I'm taking it. Your choice, muthafucka." I said walking up on him.

"Floyd, don't make me shoot yo' muthafuckin' ass. I don't fuck around with that gay shit!"

I knew he wasn't strapped because his pants were exposing everything but a gun. His ass was selling wolf tickets and I wasn't worried a bit. "Not only do you fuck around, you like how it makes you feel. Don't try to play the role with me, I know what it is. So, are we gon' do this voluntarily or what? Better yet, just take these off," I said as I grabbed the front of his pants.

"Get the fuck away from me, Floyd!"

He pushed me with all his might and I stumbled but caught myself. It only pissed me off, making me aggressive. All he had to do was comply with what I said and things would've gone smoothly. But nah, he wanted to be a hard nigga. That shit didn't last long when I yoked his ass up though.

Pressing my thumb into his throat, I pushed him up against the wall using my other hand to pull his pants down. He struggled to get out of my grip but I was stronger than his weak ass. I slung him on the bed and he kicked me in the shin.

"This is not about to happen! I will kill you, mutha-fucka!" he screamed while trying to wiggle free.

I snatched my Nina from my waist and shoved it against his temple. "Shut the fuck up and take this shit the way I know you can. Admit it, you didn't come over here to get nothing but this dick and that's what you'll get." I growled as I freed my pipe. "You bet not try to be superman in this muthafucka, this dick is gon' be your kryptonite." I laughed. Easing between his ass cheeks, I struggled to en-ter his tightness. It felt good as fuck too.

"Aaaaah, stop Floyd! You don't have to do this shit!"

This lil nigga was screaming like a bitch and that only made me want him more. I dropped my gun on the carpeted floor and opened his cheeks wide. His upper body came off the bed and I pushed him face down into the mattress and held him there as I had my way with him. The muffled sound of his screams had me ready to nut prematurely. I hit his ass with strong, deep strokes filled with anger.

"This is payback for your bitch ass brother's killing my nephew. An eye for an eye nigga. This is way better than killing yo' weak ass. You belong to me now. Every time I want this—" I said slapping his ass, "you better deliver it like Uber Eats."

Max was no longer fighting me. His body relaxed and it made it easier to get the nut I was looking for. Once I was done with him, I slid out of his hole and picked up my gun.

Walking slowly out the room, I went to the bathroom, washed up and left. He had a key, he could lock up on his way out.

"Floyd, where yo head at? I've been talking and you ain't heard shit I said." Shake said slapping me on the shoulder.

"My bad, my mind was on getting at the rest of them niggas. I know they've been looking but they won't find us. At least not the three of us."

After we sprayed the party, me, Shake, and Red fled to Memphis. I left a couple lil niggas in charge of the streets until shit died down. Mauricio was just like his daddy and he wasn't about to let shit ride without retaliating. The last thing I needed was to get caught slipping.

I sent my daughters and wife to Arizona with her people for a while. Knowing the streets the way I did, those boys would go after my family if they couldn't get to me. That's something I wouldn't be able to live with. Shake and Red were ordered to do the same but I didn't know if they did or not. I hoped they did though.

"How long do we have to stay here? Them niggas ain't coming for us, we should head back." Red said.

"You can go back if you want to, I'm not dancing with the devil right now. You look at them as youngins, I see them as the killa their daddy was. You better sit back and lay low." I warned his ass.

"Man, fuck them. I got a family back home that needs me!" Red shouted.

"I told yo' ass to relocate them! Why didn't you do that shit? You got yo' shorties and yo' bitch back in Chicago being targeted like sitting ducks! Nigga you stupid! If you didn't have the bread, I would've gave you that shit! Call and make sure everything's good with them, stupid ass."

Red had just made me mad as fuck. I didn't fuck with women and kids out in these streets. But, I knew firsthand that some niggas didn't care who died when a muthafucka murked one of their own. As Red made the call to his family, I turned toward Shake. My phone rang and Big Jim's name popped up on the screen.

"What's good, Boss?"

"Floyd, what the hell happened out there? Word got back to me that Max is dead."

"The information you received is correct. Max is dead but, he did that shit himself, Jim. He ran into the line of fire."

"What the fuck happened, Floyd? I told you not to kill him unless he started talking. Did he do that?"

"We went to Paradise Kitty because Mauricio was having a party there. We got wind of the shit when two hoes started talking about it. They didn't know we didn't fuck with them anymore and told us the location. I wanted Mauricio's head for killing John John and the respect he lacked for the organization. Max was not the target."

"Damn, I know the little nigga said some shit, but I knew he wasn't gon' out a muthafucka. Oh well, that's one down. What do you have set up to get to the rest of them?" he asked.

"We laying low right now, they gon' be out for blood, Jim."

"Fuck you mean y'all laying low? Laying low where?"

"BJ, what's up? You got me today or what?" somebody said in the background.

"Didn't I tell yo muthafuckin' ass not to call me that shit? Get the hell out until I send for yo' pussy ass! Don't ever interrupt me when I'm in the middle of handling shit!" he hissed.

Meesha

"I—"

"I nothing! Get the fuck out! Knock on my shit before you enter my house. Don't let that shit happen again!" he said dismissing whoever the person was. "I'm back. Where you at, Floyd?"

"We dipped to Memphis for a minute."

"Who the fuck is we? And who is running my shit while yo' punk ass is hiding out?"

"I'm not hiding out. Shit is hot right now and you know them lil niggas about to be gunning for us. I left Carter, Spike, and Clout in charge. You know they thorough as fuck. Things will be cool until my return. I took Shake and Red with me so we can strategize."

"You should've left one of them niggas in the Chi. Use ya head sometimes, nigga. Ricio and Sosa don't know shit about clap back, you worried for nothing. You can lay low for a few days but, I need you back to business because I need to know when the services will be. I'm coming through. I am still his guardian so all I'd have to do is pay for these pigs to get me there. But I need to know ahead of time so there won't be no bullshit."

"Aight, I got you." Was all I could say before he ended the call.

I didn't give a damn about Big Jim having an attitude. I was out here about to be playing dodge a bullet, while his ass was laid up with three hots and a cot. Fuck that, I had to figure out how to get these fools before they got me.

"What's the word, Red? Is everything okay with yo' people?" I asked giving him the evil eye.

"Yeah, they cool. I wish a muthafucka would try mine."

"Nigga, watch what you wish for. That shit might come true."

My phone rang and I looked down. Seeing Clout's name, I wondered why he would be calling so soon. I had just left him a couple hours prior. "Clout what's good, nigga?" There was silence on the other end and I got an eerie feeling that ran through my body. "Clout! Talk to me, man."

"If it was Clout, I'm sure he would've responded already. That nigga won't hold clout in the Chi no mo'. You bitch made niggas will be dropping like dominoes behind the death of my brother. Get ready because I'm picking y'all off like slaves picked cotton back in the day. Until next time, pussy." Sosa laughed as he hung up.

"Muthafucka! They got Clout. We gotta go back, they can't hold shit down without us." I yelled out.

"They are trying to bring us out, we can't give in to that, Floyd. Running into this situation blindly is not gon' be good for us. Let's get this plan together, then head back to the Chi. I know just the person that would keep their eyes and ears to the streets without being detected. Trust me on this." Shake said pulling out his phone.

I laid back on the bed thinking about the two kids that had to live without their father. That was one call I wasn't ready to make, but it had to be done. Telling Big Jim about this wasn't gon' happen. Hearing his mouth was something I wasn't looking forward to either.

Meesha

Chapter 3
Sosa

Ricio dropped me off to my car and headed home with Nija. I had every intention of going home but revenge was on my mind. All I could see was Max lying in that bed lifeless. Lying about going home to Ricio wasn't my intention. Instead of going south, I made my way to the Westside on another type of mission. As I rolled down 26th and Pulaski, it was deserted. Not a soul in sight. Doubling back to 16th and Homan, I spotted a few of Floyd's boys outside shooting craps. Not watching their surroundings as usual.

I cut my lights and sat back watching the dummies while I smoked some Kush. Pulling my fitted hat down over my eyes, I let the smoke fill up in the car. Smoking was something I tried not to do outside my home because my father always said that it impaired most people's train of thought. For me, it gave me life. I was a different muthafucka when I took it to the dome, that's when that nigga Rodrigo emerged.

Finishing off my spiff, I snubbed it out in the ashtray. I turned around in my seat and pulled the mat back on the floor in the back. The hidden compartment opened with a push of the button. I reached inside and came up with my .357 twin custom made Desert Eagles. With the thirty round extended clips, I was ready to put in work by my damn self. I grabbed the mask that I stored there and put it over my face, then put my phone in the armrest. Ricio would shit bricks if he knew I wasn't home chilling like I told him I would be. But I had shit to do and time was of the essence.

After loading both guns, I maneuvered to the passenger side and eased out the door. Gently closing it, I crept along the parked cars and ran around the block through the alley. While I sat in my whip, I noticed the block was fairly quiet and the only people out were those fools. Six of them were gambling instead of working. This was about to be too fucking easy.

Standing close to the side of the building they were in front of, I peeped around and they were still deep in their game of craps. "Pay up nigga! Seven on that ass three times in a row! I'm about to break y'all pockets tonight!" Clout yelled loudly.

"Man, it's time to change the dice! This nigga cheatin'! He winning too much!"

"Cheatin' ain't even in my blood muthafucka! Shut yo' whinny ass up and pay me my shit!" I moved quietly through the gateway seeing one of the dudes look up then stood tall. Not giving him a chance to react, I let my tool clap, hitting him in the chest with three slugs. One down five to go.

Their first mistake was freezing up instead of running. The music my pistols were singing was creating a song I would grow to love. Bodies dropped without warning and I didn't let up until everybody stopped breathing. I saw that nigga Clout laid out with blood flowing from his body like water. Without giving one fuck, I snatched his phone from his hip, and left the chump change on the ground. I glanced around and didn't see any movement on the street so I ran up the stairs to the trap and went straight for Big Jim's stash.

The game didn't change, I didn't want the bunk ass work, I only wanted the money. I filled a couple garbage bags with all the loot that was in a closet in the back bedroom. Looking around to make sure nobody was in that bitch and I bounced out the back door. When I got back in my ride, I pulled off the mask glancing in the rear view mirror. That nigga Rodrigo was smirking back at me, that was the moment I knew Sosa was pushed to the back and he had taken over.

I drove the speed limit like nothing happened because I heard sirens in the distance. Somebody heard the shots and alerted the law but I was well on my way to my crib. Stopping at a red light, I scrolled through the phone and dialed Floyd up. When he answered, I didn't say shit at first.

The second time he shouted Clout's name, I let his ass know that nigga was dead without outright saying so. But I knew he got the picture. I tossed the phone out the window as I cruised along on the expressway. Pulling into my driveway twenty minutes later, I got out and entered the house. Dropping the bags by the door and setting the alarm, I went straight to the bathroom to take a shower.

Killing them niggas didn't make me feel any better because my brother was still gone. It only meant I had to kill more to get a sigh of relief. I was all for that shit. Once I stepped out of the shower, I wrapped a towel around my waist. As I picked my pants up off the floor, I felt my phone vibrating. Jessica's name was on display and I sent her ass to voicemail. The bitch just didn't get the memo that I didn't fuck with her thieving ass.

I hadn't dropped my clothes in the hamper good before Jess was calling back. Answering her calls would never happen, she'd fucked up badly and there was no forgiveness for that. She'd better be glad I'd spared her fuckin' life and move around. If she knew what was good for her ass, she would leave me the fuck alone. This was not the time to irritate me more than I already was.

Crawling onto the bed, I scrolled through my phone and noticed Ricio had texted me to see if I made it home. I replied back telling him that I had been sleeping. It wasn't a lie because that was exactly what I was about to do. I needed to go to the club and get the footage of the shooting from Sam. He grabbed it before the police got there. Knowing exactly who shot my brother was a must. I was gon' be the one to put a bullet in their heads personally.

Sleep didn't come easily. Grabbing the remote, I turned on the tv. A rebroadcast of the news was on and the news reporter was standing outside of Paradise Kitty. I turned the volume up to see what lies them muthafuckas was speaking on about what happened.

"I'm standing in front of Paradise Kitty strip club where there was a massive shootout tonight. Two fatalities were reported and the victims were twenty-six-year-old Bernard Gilliam and eighteen-year-old Maximo Vasquez. According to witnesses, Gilliam was walking a couple ladies to their car when gunshots erupted outside of the club. He died on the scene. Vasquez was struck while trying to leave the club. He later died at the hospital. The parking lot is marked with hundreds of markings where the shell casings landed. This is one horrific scene and many want to know when the violence will end. This is Michelle Lockhart of channel seven news, back to you, Mark."

I turned the tv off and laid back on the pillow. Thoughts of Max consumed my brain and I just wanted to sleep. Lying awake for what seemed like hours, soon turned into me sitting on a park bench watching birds flying around with the sunset in the background.

"Hey, son. How are you holding up?"

Looking to my left, my heart almost stopped beating. Walking toward me was my mother, father, and Max. The words I wanted to say formulated in my mind but never reached my mouth. It was like I was star struck seeing them in front of me. My mother was as beautiful as I remembered and my father didn't look a day over thirty.

"I'm hanging in there. Shit not good, but it will be better. Max, I miss you man. I'm sorry—"

"Sosa, you have nothing to be sorry for. Everybody has a date reserved for them to leave the land of the living. It was my time to go, brah. There was nothing you could've done to prevent it. I love you and the light will shine on the situation."

The light that illuminated around the three of them was something I'd never seen before. My father walked up to me and laid his hand on my shoulder and squeezed slightly. He held his head down and when he raised it back up, the smile on his face would forever be in my mind.

"I'm proud of you and your brother, Sosa. I never wanted you boys to be involved in this street shit, but it's the hand that you were dealt. Floyd and Big Jim has to pay for what they have done in the present as well as the past. I want you to clear your head because you and Mauricio is gon' have to be on point to get back at these muthafuckas. I'm not physically able to lead y'all, but that's where Beast and Sin comes in at. I saw what you did tonight and that's what the fuck I would've done too," he laughed. "It's just the beginning, Sosa. You gotta get some security in your pocket before you produce anymore bloodshed. Get the cops in your pocket, I know them muthafuckas been grimy as fuck lately but ask Beast about the ones that rode with me. Don't let them give you no for an answer. You have enough money with more to come, money talks. Like I told Ricio, the snakes are slithering and I need y'all to watch out for 'em. We gotta get back and live our best lives. I

wanted to come down and tell you how much I love you and to make sure you good."

Gathering me in his arms, my father hugged me long and hard before he released me. My mother stepped forward and hugged me tightly. The tears cascaded down my face and I smelled the scent of her favorite body spray, cherry blossom from Bath and Body works.

"I love you Sosa. God is not ready for you yet, watch yourself out there, baby. I never wanted y'all to follow in your father's footsteps, but them two kneegrows fucked up when they fucked with my baby. I got him covered and he is alright. He is safe now, nothing will hurt him again." She said as she stepped back.

Max walked up and dapped me up like we used to do with a smile on his face. "I'm sorry I didn't tell y'all but the truth will come out. Don't try to find out what my secret was, it will come to you. I want you to know that what would be revealed will hurt you, Sosa. I want you to know I didn't ask for anything to happened the way it did. That shit was forced upon me. I love you, brah. Until we meet again." Not giving me the opportunity to respond, they all turned, walked away, and vanished into thin air.

I popped up out of my sleep and looked around my room, there was no one there but me. A single tear escaped my eye and I wiped it away. There was a message in what Max said to me and I was trying to figure out what he meant by what he said. I was going to do what he told me to do and let it come to me, but I had a feeling I wouldn't like whatever it was.

***

I didn't get much sleep after my in-dream reunion with my family. Tired was an understatement, a nigga was walking around on fumes. Drinking coffee was out of the question because that shit was nasty as fuck, I'd figure it out once I got out of the shower. Picking up my phone, I looked at the time and it was only nine o'clock. We weren't due to meet up at the warehouse until noon. There was a message from Jessie, it piqued my curiosity and I opened it.

Jessie: I wanted to send my sincere condolences to you and your family. Sorry for your loss, Sosa. If you need someone to talk to, I'm here.

This muthafucka was out of her mind. If I needed someone to talk to, it sure as hell wasn't going to be her that I ran to ass. I'd pay somebody before I dialed that bitch up. I wasn't even gon' entertain her ass with a reply, she would see that I read the message.

Walking into the bathroom to take care of my hygiene I glanced at myself in the mirror, I looked rough as fuck. My eyes were red and my five o'clock shadow was rugged as hell but I had no intention of shaving or none of that shit.

As I entered my bedroom, I looked around and went to the closet to choose my fit for the day. Staring at all the clothes I owned wasn't like any other day. My mood was dark as hell and my fit had to complement it just right. I reached in and grabbed a pair of black jeans, an all black button up shirt, and my black fitted cap. Snatching my black Timbs from the box, I turned and threw everything on the bed.

Once I oiled my body and put on my black boxers and socks, I dressed and headed downstairs to see what was in the kitchen to eat. Opening the refrigerator, I decided to actually cook something. I took out a pack of turkey bacon, a couple eggs, and milk for some waffles.

While the waffle maker was heating, I mixed the batter for four waffles then lined up a couple pieces of bacon on a pan throwing it in the oven. The silence in my crib was deafening and my mind started to wander so I grabbed the remote and turned on the surround sound.

"Alexa, play 90's rap." I said out loud. "Niggaz done started something" by DMX blared through the speakers. Bobbing my head to the beat, I prepared my meal while rapping along. This song didn't do nothing but put me back in killa mode and I was lovin' that shit

If you love the money, then prepare to die for it
Niggas done started something
You can lay in the flames, or hold the sky for it
Niggas done started something.
Don't come for me with no bullshit, use caution
Cause when I wet shit, I dead shit, like abortions
For bigger portions, of extortion then racketeering
Got niggas fearing, fuck what you heard, this what you hearing
How much darker must it get, how much harder must it hit
See if your hardest niggas flip, when I start a bunch of shit
I like pussy, but not up in my face, so gimme three feet

X was speaking to me and hardening my soul. The shit in my head had me ready to go out and lose my mutha-fuckin' mind. I finished making my breakfast and sat at the island gobbling it down. After drinking a tall glass of orange juice, I was full and ready to go back to sleep. I had moves to make so that wasn't happening. Heading upstairs, I heard my phone ringing. Taking the steps two at a time, I caught the call before the voicemail picked up.

"Holla at me." I said into the phone without checking the caller ID.

"Where the fuck is my money, muthafucka?" I laughed into the phone because this nigga must've been crazy as hell to dial my phone. "I don't see shit funny, bitch. I want my shit and I want it now. You killed six of my men and you laughing!"

"Hell yeah! I'm laughing because yo' hoe ass killed my brother. One life from me means all y'all lives don't matter. Be ready to lose plenty more of your people because it won't stop until every last one of y'all stop breathing. It's game time and oh, as far as your money goes, that shit belongs to me now." I said hanging up on his punk ass.

Checking the time, I noticed it was almost eleven o'clock. I grabbed my keys and tucked my bitch in my pants and hit the door. Shit was about to get real in Chicago.

Meesha

Chapter 4
Mauricio

Last night was a night to remember and not in a good way. Keeping an eye on Sosa was something I was going to have to put as top priority. He wasn't taking the death of Max well at all, he wouldn't even go into the room to say his goodbyes. Bruh told me he was going home to sleep but in the back of mind, I should've followed him.

Nija was a mess and I just wanted to get her to my house and hold her. Losing Max took a toll on my baby and I didn't need her breaking down on me. Planning a funeral was something I'd never thought I would have to do at the age of twenty-one. I didn't know where to start. To be honest, in my mind I wouldn't have to because my baby brother would be ringing the bell bright and early.

When I pulled into the garage of my condo, Nija had her eyes closed with tears running out the corners. I parked my car and looked down at my clothes. The blood that was in my pants couldn't be seen, but I could smell it. Instantly the vision of my brother getting hit with multiple bullets invaded my mind.

My hands balled into fists tightly and the urge to kill overtook my body. I silently willed myself to calm down and relax. Looking over at Nija, my heart ached for her. As I turned the car off the sound of her crying filled the space. The small shake of her shoulders could be seen and I knew she was about to come undone.

I reached over and gathered her in my arms, lifting her over the console so she was nestled in my lap. "It's okay, Ni. Max is alright now. We will not mourn him, but we will celebrate his life so he will never be forgotten. I want to thank you for always being there for him, for all of us in our times of need. I will always love you for that," I whispered in her ear.

"There's no need for you to thank me, Ricio. Y'all welcomed me with open arms and allowed me to become a part of the family. Max was the little brother I never had and I am going to miss his hardheaded ass." she sniffled.

"Yeah, he didn't listen for shit, but that was Max for you. Now he will be our guardian angel and he's gonna look after us . Stop all that crying, we have to plan this funeral some way or another. Are you down to help me with this shit, Ni?"

"Sin and I are going to plan everything. The only thing we want is you and Sosa's input. All I want you to do is prepare your mind, Ricio. This is about to take you back to four years ago, but worse. Do you follow me?"

"I know. This is about to be one long ass week and I can't prepare myself for this shit. I should've—"

"Nope, that's what you're not going to do, blame yourself. You and Sosa have to get that out y'all heads. Looking for a reason to kill is not the answer. Y'all are going to do that shit anyway. Big Jim and Floyd are the reason shit got started, finish it. I just want you to have all your ducks in a row and come back to me. My head hurts and I'm done talking about this for now," she stated getting out of the car.

Following her lead, I did the same and hit the alarm button. The elevator doors opened and Nija stepped inside leaning against the wall. I pushed the button to my floor and waited. She didn't waste anytime going down the hall and unlocking the door once we exited the elevator, she didn't even wait to walk with me. As I locked the door, I could hear the shower running when I got close to the bedroom.

Nija wasn't in the room so I knew where to find her. Entering the bathroom, I could see her silhouette through the glass shower doors. Her hands were braced against the wall and the water was running over her head. The steam was thick so I knew the water was extremely hot. She was trying her best to suppress her cries, but I heard them.

Peeling my bloodstained clothes from my body, I tossed them in the corner because I was burning all that shit as soon as I had Nija settled in bed. I slid the door open and she didn't even raise her head. All I could do was wrap my arms around her waist and hold her. The water at my feet was a light pink color from the dried-up blood that was on my legs. I prayed Nija didn't open her eyes because she would go crazy.

"Let it all out, Ni. Cry enough for me because I don't have any more tears to let out," I said as I reached around her and grabbed her body wash and loofah.

Lathering the loofah, I started washing her body from head to toe. Sitting her on the bench, I quickly washed myself and got out. The plush towel that I wrapped around my waist felt good against my skin and I felt sleepiness coming over me.

"Step out, Ni." I said softly as I held the towel open.

She walked into my arms and I wrapped the towel around her body and cradled her in my arms. Carrying her into the bedroom, I placed Nija in the bed and covered her. I eased in the bed behind her and rocked her until her light snores were heard. I kissed her on her forehead and slid my arm from under her head.

"Where are you sneaking off to, Ricio? Please don't leave this house tonight," she spoke quietly without opening her eyes.

"I promise I'm not going out. I have to make sure Sosa got home safely and I also have to call my uncle in the Dominican Republic. The balcony is where I'll be, love."

Kissing her cheek, I grabbed a pair of basketball shorts, a sleeveless shirt and a pair of socks out of the dresser. After dressing I went to my stash and grabbed of bag of purp and a blunt. Nija was stirring in her sleep but she didn't wake up. I scooped up my phone and a lighter and headed for the balcony.

Sosa should've been home by now so I sent him a text to make sure. He didn't reply after fifteen minutes and I was ready to ride down on his ass. I was going to give him a minute to hit me back before I went looking for his ass.

I stared at my phone for a spell before I scrolled through to my uncle Alejandro's name. My thumb hoovered over his contact info for a couple minutes without pressing it. Talking to my mother's side of the family was something I haven't done in four years. Them muthafuckas were foul as fuck and I didn't like fucking with them.

As much as I didn't want to make this call, it was unavoidable. My mother's brothers hadn't been in contact with us since the day of her funeral. They didn't bother showing up to pay respect for papí because they didn't have none for him. Nobody in that family approved of the fact my mother married outside her race. Papí dealt with the shit that they said because her family had a right to their opinion. That's all the fuck it was and they knew not to voice that shit in his face.

Everything that was said went straight to mommy and the only way papí found out was if he saw mommy crying. He checked their asses on many occasions and they eventually stop bringing the shit to mommy because they were afraid of what papí would do. Reese didn't give a fuck who you were, if you disrespected his wife, that was your head.

I finally clicked on Alejandro's name. As I listened to the phone ring, the urge to hang up was strong. When I was about to end the call, it was answered on the other end. "Hola, Mauricio. Es trade, ¿Como está todo?" (Hello, Mauricio. It's late, how's everything?) Alejandro asked sleepily.

I was trying to find the right words to say but nothing came to mind. There wasn't an easy way to tell him that Max was gone. I just couldn't form the words to do so.

"¿Que pasa, sobrino?" (What's wrong, nephew?) he asked. I heard him shuffling around before the sound of his house shoes dragging on the floor was heard.

"Maximo—Maximo fue asesinado esta noche." (Maximo was killed tonight.)

The silence on the other end of the line was deathly quiet. I didn't say anything. The tears were falling from my eyes rapidly. Speaking those words out loud made everything real. My heart was shattered because I was supposed to protected him and I didn't.

"Apuesto a que era algorithm que tenia que ver con see padre negro cult tuyo!" (I bet it was something that had to do with that black ass father of yours!) He had the nerve to say. "Debí seguir mi primera mente u traerlos de Vuelta a la República Domimicana después de que mi hermana muriera." (I should've followed my first mind and brought you boys back to the Dominican Republic after my sister died.)

I didn't like the things he said and I damn sure didn't like his tone. The only thing I wanted to do was let him know what went down with Max. He turned this into a whole other thing talking bad about papí. He pissed me off so bad I went straight hood on his ass.

"First of all, Alejandro, you wouldn't be bumpin' yo' gums if that same nigga you talking down about was walking this earth. Let's make sure things are clear around this bitch, I demand the same mufuckin' respect! I won't sit back and let you say shit that's not valid. If you thought the words you spoke was gon' get some play, you thought wrong! Watch ya fuckin' mouth! Secondly, in the eyes of every damn body, you are the same nigga that yo' ass despises to this day. Dominicans ain't no different than black people, we ain't respected by the white people on the same mufuckin' level, nigga! So, when you come for Reese, put respect on his name, bitch! I didn't have to call and tell you shit about what happened to my brother. Out of respect is why I did. You just blew the fuck outta me. I'll let you know when and where the services will be held. If you show up, great. If not, fuck you too!" I banged on his ass without allowing him the opportunity to respond.

Alejandro Vasquez had a lot to learn about me, I just wasn't about to be the righteous teacher to school his ass. The next time he came at me like a little ass kid, I was blowing his shit back. Uncle or not, he chose the wrong time to fuck with me.

Flaming up the Kush I rolled while chewing out my uncle, I took that shit to the head. It was fire if I should say so myself. I needed to hit Fife up to tell him I would be coming through solo to cop some of this shit for the operation. Floyd won't be needing his services after a while.

I finished the blunt and I felt a little better and was ready to go to sleep. Making my way back to my bedroom, I crawled in the bed and put my phone on the nightstand. As soon as I turned to cuddle with Ni, I got a text message alert. Grabbing the phone, I saw it was Sosa letting me know he was sleeping and he was home. My body relaxed knowing that my brother was good, I fell sleep with no problem at all.

***

Nija's ass was all over my bed when I woke up. A big ass king sized bed was just half of a twin for me. Her ass wasn't even that damn big to be hogging the entire damn bed. Looking over at her, I instantly forgot what I was mad about. She was spread eagle with the sheet covering only her stomach. My mouth watered at the sight of her clean shaved kitty.

Scooting to the foot of the bed, I moved the sheet a little and crept between her legs that were inviting me to a buffet in bed. Sex should've been the last thing on my mind but that wasn't the case. I placed my mouth against her mound and licked her lower lips. She stirred slightly but not enough to wake up.

I used my fore finger and thumb to open her lips revealing her pink center. Her pearl stood at attention and I wrapped my lips around it sucking softly. Holding her thighs with a strong grip, I went wild on her clit. Nija's legs started trembling but she still didn't fully wake up. Using my tongue to penetrate her wetness, her eyes fluttered.

"Oh shit." She moaned softly. Her hips rocked back and forth against my mouth allowing me to lock down on her bud once more. "Right there, baby! I'm about to cum!"

Before I knew what was going on, she had my head locked against her pussy while she fed me. I didn't complain because it was all about pleasing her. Letting her body relax so she could start her day refreshed. Nija was thrusting her hips hard and fast and I had a vice grip on her pearl.

41

She was panting like she was having contractions. Her clit hardened and her legs locked in place as she squirted all her sweet nectar down my throat.

"Aaaaahhhh! Fuck, Ricio don't stop! Suck it harder, daddy. I feel another one coming and I want it!" she moaned as she rocked against my mouth.

Shifting my body to adjust my joint because he was harder than a mufucka, I stuck two fingers into her love box and found her gspot. The fuck faces Ni was making were turning me on even more than I already was. My finger tips found the spot I was seeking and I gave her the best internal massage one could give with two fingers.

"Oh my gosh that feels so fucking good! I need that dick to get this one Ricio. Fuck me please, baby."

She didn't have to tell my black ass twice. Removing my mouth from her lower lips, I kept my fingers inside her and moved up her body to kiss her tenderly. Our tongues wrestled together hungrily and my pipe was ready to explore her silky center. Releasing my fingers, I rubbed against her wetness with my mushroom head.

"Mmmmmm" she moaned as she pushed forward.

I was just as eager as she was but I wanted to take my time. Slowly entering her, the wetness coated my Johnson and I thought I had died and went to heaven it felt so good. Rocking my hips back and forth I caught a rhythm and lifted her legs above her head. With all the frustrations I had inside of me, I let it out on her kitty.

"Oh shit!" she moaned loudly clawing at my back.

I felt every scratch that she applied and it burned like hell but that didn't stop me from giving her what she and I both wanted. Burying my face in the crook of her neck, I fucked her nice and slow. When I felt her sugary wall close around me, I knew she was about to cum hard. Speeding up my stroke, I grabbed her ass with both hands and went in deeper. The tip of my dick kept hitting her gspot repeatedly and I felt all my unborns swimming to the top.

"Shit, Ni! This pussy good, baby," I murmured against her ear. "You love me?"

"Yes, I love you, Ricio." She purred back.

That's all I needed to hear before I let my load go into her womb. "Aaaaaaah, yeah!" I groaned loudly.

"Yessssss, mmmmmmm." She sighed closing her eyes.

I rolled over and she nestled against me and fell back into a deep sleep. I looked at the time on the clock on the nightstand and I had an hour to dress and make it to the warehouse. Kissing her on the temple, I got out of bed to start my day.

Meesha

Chapter 5
Beast

Seeing Max lying in that hospital bed motionless did something to me. The mixed emotions that I was experiencing had me heated one minute and emotional the next. I'm a hard muthafucka to break but this shit right here, had a nigga almost crumbling. Only for a millisecond though. My mind has been on death since I walked out of that hospital and saw Sosa falling apart and blaming himself for what the fuck happened.

I knew first hand how it felt to blame yourself for something that was out of your control. Not being there for Reese on that dreadful night took over my soul for years and almost destroyed me. Max getting killed and I was right there, should've hit me harder but it didn't. Why? Because that nigga did that shit purposely.

The way he was throwing back those shots told me everything I needed to know. I had just got up to go holla at him when I saw that nigga Floyd step in the club. Puling my phone out I gave Ricio and Sosa a heads up and made my way to Max. Before I could get through the crowd, everyone was going for the door. All I remember was hearing gunshots coming from outside and Max bolting for the door.

"Erique, come eat!"

Breaking me from my thoughts, Sin was screaming through my shit like she was the boss of me. "Why are you screaming, Sincere?' I asked walking slowly down the stairs.

"We have shit to do today, that's why."

As I entered the kitchen, Sin had a plate of bacon, grits, eggs, and toast waiting for me on the table along with a cup of java. She was standing by the microwave with a big ass cake bowl but I knew damn well she wasn't making no cake. I sat down and stared at her because curiosity was getting the best of me.

"Sin, what the fuck is in that bowl and where is your plate?"

"I'm not eating that shit, Erique! This *is* my breakfast right here," she sassed.

"That's not telling me what's in the bowl though."

"It's oatmeal, nosey."

The fork that was halfway to my mouth dropped to the plate. I knew damned well she didn't have a big ass cake bowl full of oatmeal when she could've just eaten what she cooked for me. Scooting the chair back, I walked over to where she was standing and peeked in the bowl.

"Sin, please explain to me why you have a pack of instant oatmeal in this big ass bowl."

"For your information, Beast, there's two packs of oatmeal in this bowl," she stated rolling her eyes.

"It still doesn't make sense for you to have that big ass bowl though. Why couldn't you make the shit in this bowl?" I asked taking a smaller bowl from the cabinet.

"I wanted to use this muthafucka right here! Now, sit down and eat your food so we can get out of here. Today is not the day for you to be trying to piss me off. Regardless of the fact, *we* are going to the warehouse, you can stop trying to get under my skin because it won't work."

Sin stomped over to the table and plopped down in the chair eating her strawberry and cream oatmeal out of that big ass bowl. I followed suit and dug into my grits and eggs. After a moment of silence, I looked across the table and took in her beauty. She didn't look a day over twenty-five and she was all of forty-six. My bitch was bad and none of these young hoes had shit on her.

"Tell me this, why do you want to go to the warehouse so badly?"

"Really, Beast?" She asked leaning her head to the side. "Do you not remember what the fuck transpired last night? I refuse to sit back and let my nephews tackle this shit alone."

"They not tackling nothing alone! They got me!" I yelled cutting her off. "I don't want you back in the game, Sin. Let us handle this shit, please."

"I respect you on so many levels and usually I would bow down when you speak, but there isn't a damned thing you can say to stop me from getting in on this. You want to get mad at me for my decision, do that. But I will be right by your side to handle these pussy muthafuckas. Max didn't deserve whatever the fuck made him run into the line of fire last night. I've tried my best to figure out what's been eating that child up for years. He always said he was alright. Max started getting deep into the streets right after Reese died. It didn't have shit to do with him chasing a dollar, Beast. He has been hurting from something else and I'm determined to find out what it is."

"I tried talking to him too but he wasn't talking! I'm not talking about Max right now, I'm worried about you trying to get back into the streets! I don't want you to get hurt behind this shit, Sin. Shit is different than back in the day. I love you and I would die if something happened to you."

"I love you too, Beast. You don't have to worry about me because you know first hand that I can hold my own. Being out of the game and walking around this muthafucka cooking, cleaning, and fucking yo' ass got you thinking

I'm this domesticated ass bitch. I'm all that and more, but these bitches killed my baby, Beast!" she cried out as she threw the bowl across the room. "I'm willing to die behind this one and I'm taking as many muthafuckas with me that I can. I'm not sitting this shit out. I owe that much to Reese and Maritza," she said getting up walking out of the kitchen.

Trying to finish my breakfast, I thought about what Sin said. Talking her out of going with me would only make her go out on her own to do what she wanted to do. I didn't want that at all. The best thing for me to do was to let her roll with the crew. Sin never cried so I knew she was hurting. With this level of hurt from her, death wasn't too far behind.

The food on my plate was cold as hell and I had lost my appetite. Taking a sip of my coffee, it was nice and hot so I settled on that being breakfast. I finished up, threw the food away, and rinsed my dishes before putting them in the dishwasher. After cleaning up the mess Sin made, I said a silent prayer before heading upstairs to get dressed.

I handled my hygiene and threw on a pair of jeans with my Notre Dame jersey and a pair of wheat colored Tims. As I placed my Notre Dame fitted on my head, Sin walked in. The all white pantsuit she wore hugged her body just right. The open toed stilettos that graced her feet showed off her pretty toes. Her makeup was flawless and she didn't look like she was going to a meeting to discuss a get back strategy.

"Sin, you are not dressed for the warehouse, babe. This place hasn't been used in years. It's gon' be dirty as fuck in there."

"Erique I don't go anywhere looking like an average bitch. This is something you already know about me. I will slit a nigga's throat in a mini dress and it wouldn't change the fact that his ass was dead. That goes for these mutha-fuckas too," she said revealing her twin silver and chrome Nina's that were hiding under her jacket.

Sin City was out for blood full blown and I didn't like it. I'd stopped all of my dealings in the streets to put this side of her to rest. Life has brought her back out and there was no turning back from it. Grabbing my keys, I looked at her and shook my head. "We don't have too much time to waste, let's get out of here," was all I could say before I walked out the door.

In the car I turned the radio up and smooth jazz filled the car. We were cruising on the highway when my phone started ringing. I glanced down seeing Chuck's name dis-played on the screen and hit the button on the steering wheel to answer the call.

"Chuck, what's up?"

"Aye, I just saw on the news that Max was killed last night. My condolences, Big Dawg."

"Thanks, man. The shit is wild but it's all good. I want you to keep an eye on that nigga Big Jim behind them walls. His crew did that shit and his days are numbered," I said merging into the next lane.

"I got him. You think he had something to do with this?" Chuck asked.

"I know the muthafucka had everything to do with it. How has he been acting?"

"That I don't know because I didn't learn about the shit until this morning on the news. I'm working the mid shift today, though. I'll see where his mind is when I get there. He is always trying to talk to me about the outside but I told his ass I'm not with that shit no mo'."

"Yeah, keep that shit on the low. Get that nigga to trust you because you are back on the payroll. We out to bring down his entire operation and he will lose his life in the process. I need you to get into his files and get me his lawyer's information and a copy of his case. I have to make sure I know what's going on just in case his ass gets off somehow."

"I got you, Dawg. I'm ready for whatever. You know how it used to be when Reese was still around, murder on deck."

"That's what the fuck I'm talking about! Keep me posted on everything you find out. I have a meeting to attend so I'll holla at ya later." I said disconnecting the call.

I drove down 127th street with a lot of shit on my mind. I was so zoned out that I didn't realize I had run a red light. Car horns blared and I had to swerve to miss a car that I almost ran into.

"Beast! What the fuck!" Sin screamed at me. "You have to clear your head, I want to live to see another fucking day. Do you want me to drive?"

"No, I got this, I'm sorry baby. I'm focused."

"You better be, shit."

Making a right onto Halsted Street, I cruised the speed limit thinking about how we were about to handle this beef. The text message tone on my phone chimed indicating I had a text message. "See who that is, baby." Sin picked up my phone and read the message.

"It's Mauricio and he wants to know where you at. I responded that we would be there in less than ten minutes."

"Thanks. We will be there in less time than that, we're only up the street."

When I pulled up to the warehouse, Ricio, Sosa, Psycho, Felon, Face, and AK were shooting the shit in the parking lot. I parked my whip and stepped out and made my way over to them. There was an U-Haul truck parked next to Ricio's car and I knew he came ready to get shit going.

"What's up, muthafuckas? Y'all ready to put everything on the table or what?" I asked dapping up everybody.

"Hell yeah—" Ricio started to say then stopped. "Damn Sin! What I tell you about shittin' on these bitches out here! Yo ass is finer than wine, ma." He said walking toward her with a little too much swag.

I pulled his ass back by his shirt with force, "what the fuck I tell you about coming on to my woman, nigga?"

"Damn, Beast, it ain't even like that. You shouldn't have the baddest bitch in the Chi on yo' team. I'm gon' forever give credit where it's due when I see Sin. Witcho hatin' ass," Ricio said snatching away with his arms outstretched. "Come here, girl and gimme a hug."

"Hey, Ricio. You better stop playing with that man's emotions before he shoots yo' ass," she laughed. "How are you holding up?" Sin asked stepping out of his embrace and walked over hugging my waist.

"I'm chillin'. I can't say the last twenty something hours have been great, you know under different circumstances maybe." He said hunching his shoulders.

"Sosa, you good, baby?" She asked. He didn't answer, in fact he kept looking down at his phone. Everybody was looking at him because he acted like Sin hadn't said his name at all. "Sosa, are you alright?"

Ricio was looking at him through squinted eyes and I stalked toward Sosa because the disrespect was not about to happen with my woman. Ricio held up his hand for me to stop and shook his head. I stopped in my tracks and waited to see what would happen next.

"Rodrigo, Sin asked are you good, brah," Ricio said softly.

His head snapped up and his eyes were dark and emotionless. He paused and looked at Sin, "nah, I'm not gon' front and say I am when I'm not. But enough of this shit, I'm ready to get rolling so we can get at these niggas. Beast, open the door so we can get shit in motion," he said walking toward the door to the warehouse.

"Who the fuck is Rodrigo?" Beast asked.

"I'll explain that shit later, Unc. Let's handle this business," Ricio said as he joined Sosa or Rodrigo—whoever the fuck he was.

Chapter 6
Mauricio

Sosa's mind was in another place. The very first time Rodrigo showed up was when he was about ten years old. Sosa fell off the jungle gym in the park trying to do a back flip off it. He hit his head pretty hard. Mom took him to the hospital and the doctor's told her he had a really bad concussion and some of his brain activity wasn't normal.

After running a lot of tests, the waves miraculously went back to normal. They couldn't figure out what was going on and sent him home. He was fine a few days later and back to normal when the knot went down. One day a kid at school was bullying him and he snapped. Sosa beat the kid's ass and put him in the hospital with a broken leg. He snapped his leg in two with his bare hands. The principle was trying to get him locked up in juvenile detention, but he'd never been in trouble before.

I saw a difference in his eyes and his mannerisms weren't the same. It was like he was a different person but it went away within a few hours and he was back to his old self. But when papí and ma died, he changed up again. One of Big Jim's workers was always short when he brought in his take. He pulled a gun on Sosa and before anyone could react, the dude's head was rolling across the floor.

Sosa wiped the machete off on his dark pants and put it back in the holster on his leg. Rodrigo was around for a few months before Sosa emerged again. Now he was back and nobody on the opposing team was safe. Beast was sitting at the head of the table and the meeting began when we were all seated.

"First things first, thank ya'll for showing up today. Everybody in this building has agreed to be here by being in attendance. Shit is about to be a bloody mess and I want to make sure ya'll know that your lives are at stake." There were nods all around the table including Sin's. "Okay, word on the street is that Floyd and his two haven't been seen since last night. We have to make them niggas come out of hiding." Beast said folding his hands in front of him.

"I already kicked that off, they should be back real soon." Rodrigo said sinisterly.

Heads turned in his direction but he looked straight ahead at nothing in particular. "What do you mean by that, Sosa?" Beast asked.

"Hey Beast, no disrespect, fam but my name is Rodrigo. I would really appreciate if you address me as such. To answer your question, I took care of six of them niggas last night on 16th street. Clout was one of them. I called that nigga Floyd and let him know that his crew was on my radar." He said nonchalantly.

"I thought you said you were going straight to the crib last night, bro." Sosa had never lied to me about his whereabouts. With the shit we had going on, this was not the time to waver on that shit.

Chuckling, he stared at me, "Sosa told you that bullshit, I had other plans. I may not come out often, but Max was my brother too. I'm not about to make this shit easy for these muthafuckas. Their families are about to cry like Sosa did last night. I was glad when his tear ducts dried up, it gave me the opportunity to push my way to the front. You of all people know how I get down. If I'm out, that means I brought hell with me. Enough about me, Beast, I was told to ask you about the pigs that my father had on his payroll. I need them muthafuckas asap. I can't kill until I get that shit set up and my trigga finger is itchin'.""

Rodrigo was calm and I knew murder was the only thing on his mind. Beast had a look of confusion on his face but it disappeared quickly. "I'll get on that pronto, is there anything else you need before I get back to business?

"Yeah, I want to be in on the meeting with the pigs. I was told not to take no for an answer, so I want to make sure that doesn't happen," he smirked.

"So, who is giving you all of these demands?" Psycho asked.

"Who the fuck else other than Reese, nigga." Rodrigo sneered back.

"Now I know yo' ass done lost yo' muthafuckin' mind." Psycho laughed.

Rodrigo jumped up and snatched Psycho by the collar before he could get the entire ha ha out his mouth. His quick action cut that shit short. "Don't ever in your muthafuckin' life call me crazy! Ain't shit crazy about me! I'll snatch yo' muthafuckin' head off. You lucky yo' ass is needed and you mean a lot to my brother. Check ya'self from this point, don't let that shit happen again."

"Let him go, brah. He didn't know. Sit down, Rodrigo."

Releasing Psycho's shirt, he sat down and pulled out a blunt. "Ya'll mind if I blow something other than this nigga's brains out?" Rodrigo asked without waiting for a reply.

After we watched my brother smoke half of his spiff, Beast started speaking again. "I have someone on the inside watching Big Jim. I will have his case file in my possession soon. I will get the information on his lawyer and spook the fuck out of whoever is representing that nigga. The warden is also on my list of people to holla at. I have a few kinks to work out with that plan, as soon as I have everything ironed out, I'll let y'all know what's up."

"Okay, that sounds like a plan. Who is the muthafucka that you got on the inside, Beast? Whoever it is needs to befriend that nigga and get close to him. I met a lil cutie in there when I went for my visit. I'm gon' see what she can find out," I shared with them.

"I don't think you should involve some bitch you really don't know. You have no idea what type of shit that hoe may be on. Shid, she may be on that nigga's team already. Don't let ya dick think for you right now, Ricio. That hoe would be history trying to play a game she knows nothing about." Sin said staring at her nails.

"Sin is right, don't include anyone new in this shit. The person I have on the inside has been riding with us since back in the day. I trust him with my life. Big Jim don't know that he is still part of the family so he will go unde-tected without suspicion." Beast added his two cents.

Maybe they were right and I was going to respect what they said. Latorra would still be on the back burner just in case. "Okay, I'll leave that alone. What are we gon' do about the storage locker? I know we can't get to the bank until Monday, but we need to transfer that merchandise here today. I already got the truck to transport that shit."

"We will take care of that when we are finished here and I peeped that when I pulled up. Sin, has the hospital called about Madysen?" Beast asked.

"Yes, she was placed under suicide watch. I will be heading to the hospital once I get back to my car. The doc-tor wants to talk to me about her prognosis."

"When we leave here, we will be going to the storage facility then back here. The cleaning crew will be here soon to get this place cleaned up while we're gone. I want you to take my ride and head to the hospital. The way it sounds, Madysen needs us. She had no one but Max, so we are her family now. Let's talk about the arrangements. Sin when will you and Nija get on that?" Beast asked.

"Nija is working on things while I'm here. I will meet up with her once I finish checking on Madysen."

"Okay, do that. I don't want to hear about that shit, right now!" Rodrigo yelled. "What else needs to be addressed as far as the murders of my fuckin' family?" Rodrigo wanted to know. "All that other shit ain't what I want to hear about. I'm ready to kill got dammit!"

"Calm all that shit down, Rodrigo! You just killed six muthafuckas—"

"And I wanna kill twenty mo'!" he said cutting me off.

"Aight, I was thinking about the black impala them niggas was rollin' in last night. I've seen that car before." I said glancing at Psycho trying to see any signs of deception.

"Why are looking at me like that, Ricio. I don't know shit about that vehicle."

"I had a dream that took me back to the night my father was murdered. That was the same car that was on the scene that night. The funny thing about, I knew who the driver was. That same person was the one that ran up behind my father and shot him in the head." I sat back watching his reaction and he still looked clueless to what I was saying. It was obvious he didn't know where I was going with what I said, so I kept going. "I didn't want to believe what my dreams revealed but they had been on point thus far. My father left me a recording letting me in on all the muthafuckas that were on his shit list and who was working with them. Big Jim let me know that his part in the shit was true, along with Floyd's ass. Now, there was a name that was mentioned that I wouldn't believe until I saw for myself.

That brings me to you, Psycho." I paused for a second, giving him the chance to speak.

"Ricio, you and me were the same muthafuckin' age. I didn't know shit about Big Jim back in the day. Basketball was what I was into, right along with yo' ass. I'm not taking the fall for that shit! I didn't have nothing to do with that. Reese was like a second father to me!" He screamed jumping up.

"Sit yo' ass down, Psych! Ricio, where the hell you going with this?" Beast asked without taking his eyes off Psycho.

"I don't know how this shit gon' play out but the muthafucka behind the wheel of that Impala was Rodney." I said.

"Rodney who?" Psycho asked with his eyebrow raised.

"Yo' muthafuckin daddy, nigga!" I yelled back at his ass.

"I don't believe that shit for one minute! My daddy is a prestigious lawyer and he ain't never been a street nigga. You got your information wrong on this one, brah," he said shaking his head.

"Psych, what you said is far from the truth. I know for a fact your daddy ran with Big Jim and Floyd back in the day. He was one of their top soldiers. Reese never told me that he had any beef with Rod but I'm quite sure he disclosed that shit to Ricio."

"As a matter of fact, I recorded that part on my phone for this purpose right here," I said reaching for my phone on my hip. I went to the voice memo app and selected the recording. I pressed play and sat the phone on the table turning the volume all the way up. Reese's voice flowed through the phone.

"I don't know if you and Sosa still hang around Fred, but what I'm about to say may mess up ya'll friendship. Rodney was in on the shit with Big Jim and Floyd. The reason I didn't disclose that information on the other recording is because I want you to see what your friend knows. I want you to test his loyalty to you and have him confront his bitch ass father about the situation. That will let you know where you stand with him."

"I don't know shit about that, Ricio. I swear to God!" Psycho said holding his right hand up.

"Truthfully speaking, fam, I believe you. This was your father's doing and I wouldn't lie about seeing him before I even listened to this recording. So, there's a lot of truth to it. Like my daddy said, this is where you prove your loyalty to not just me, but to the team." I explained to him.

"What do you expect me to say to my pops?" Psycho asked.

"Whatever the fuck you need to! That muthafucka pulled the trigga and he has been added to the muthafuckin' list, nigga! What happened to 'There's no turning back from this. They killed my brother and I swear, every one of them muthafuckas are gon' feel this heat. I don't give a fuck who wasn't there, all them niggas getting it?' Your words, nigga and that goes for your punk ass daddy too!" Rodrigo said pounding on the table. "Ricio is trying to reason with yo ass. You been around our family forever and I consider you a brother but that won't stop me from putting one in yo' dome. Your daddy is your responsibility and it's up to you to handle his ass. Daddy or not, if his explanation don't measure up, you end that muthafucka or you will have to answer to me!"

"Psycho this is part of the game, youngin. All I can say is bring up Max's situation and go from there. Obviously,

Rod got a past life that he has kept away from you. He wanted you to look at him as the lawyer that he is today and not the thug he was back in then. You will have to use the street smarts you possess to get him to open up." Beast chimed in.

"There's no other way. If one of us goes to your daddy, after he reveals what we want to know, he's gonna die. Plain and simple. You have a chance to get the information from him and he may still live. Your choice," Sin said sitting up in her chair. "I'm a lot different from the girl I was back then, I can easily get close to Rod and make him think pussy is what he would get, but he would be dead within a half hour."

"Aight, I'm on it. Y'all know this is putting me between a rock and a hard place. This is my father."

"Reese was my muthafuckin' daddy too but that didn't stop that nigga from putting a slug in the back of his muthafuckin' head! I'd advise yo' ass to get the shit done and come back with some lucrative information, fam. Next topic." Rodrigo said dismissing the subject.

My head was started to hurt a little bit. I pinched the bridge of my nose and closed my eyes. I didn't know how stressful this shit would be. "Okay, there is another situation that I have to handle. Reese wants me to find Slim and clean him up. What's his story, Beast? I'm trying to get all the information that I was given out. All of this shit plays a major part in the shit that's going on."

"Slim was the moneymaker of our crew. He fell hard after Reese got murdered. Instead of selling the product that was left to him by your father, most of it went into his veins. He was broke within a year, living on the streets and a full fledge crackhead. I tried to get him help but he didn't want it. He always said without Reese he was nothing.

When you find him, make him go, don't give him a choice. Throw your daddy in his face if you have to. Reese wanted you to get him right, there's a reason behind everything he has in place." Beast said.

"Bet, I'm on that shit today. Is there anything else we need to discuss?" I asked.

"There is something that has been bothering me. I've been trying to piece together the shit that happened on 79th when you were shot at, Ricio." Sin said while glancing at me.

"I never told ya'll about that. How do you know?"

"Just know that I know. Who knew where you were, other than Nija?" she asked.

"Nobody that I know of. If you are implying Nija had something to do with this, Sin, you are wrong."

"One thing I know is Nija is thorough when it comes to your ass, Ricio. She needs to leave your ass alone until you get right, but that ain't my business. She will never do you wrong. I will ask her about that day from her viewpoint, something ain't adding up."

"Do that, Sin. Oh, I talked to Alejandro last night and I had to tell him the fuck off. I don't know if he will be coming to the service, but if he does, he better have a different approach."

"Don't tell me that nigga still hating on Reese and he ain't even here anymore?" Beast laughed.

"Yeah, he is. He is bound to get his ass beat if he comes to the states trying to be hard. One of y'all better inform his ass that Reese lives within me, literally." I laughed.

"Ain't that the truth. He hasn't seen you in years and he is in for a world of surprise. He gon' think he saw a ghost when he lays eyes on yo' big ass." Sin laughed.

"I guess we have covered everything. Let's get to this storage unit, we have things to do." Beast said glancing at his phone. "The clean up crew is here, right on time too. One more thing, has anyone reached out to Butta's family?"

"I went over to his mom's house last night and told them before the news broadcasted. His mom is going through it as well as his baby mama. I let them know that we would be back over with the money for his services. Shantell said she would let me know the date and the amount, he didn't have insurance." Felon said.

"All the muthafuckin' money that nigga made in the street and he didn't think to make sure his shit was good with the job that he had. I hope the rest of you niggas are covered as well as your kids." Beast preached as he went to let the cleaners in.

"Psycho, you good, fam?" I asked as I watched him stare off in space.

"Yeah, I'm good. All of the shit with my dad is a surprise. He always criticized me about what I did in the street and he ain't no better than me. I know how I will approach the situation, don't worry I got this, Ricio."

"I hope so," Rodrigo said walking up slapping Psycho on the shoulder. "Let me know if you need me to step in, I'm ready to kill a muthafucka." He said walking away.

Shaking my head as I watched him light another blunt. I didn't know what the fuck I was going to do about his ass, I wanted to beat the shit out of him like the priest did to Reagan in the *Exorcist.* I need Sosa to come back before this nigga got himself locked the fuck up.

Chapter 7
Latorra

I had to work late last night and when I got home, I fell out after showering. When I woke up it was damn near two in the afternoon. I got things together for my Saturday cleaning session. Turning the television on in the living room, as I headed to the kitchen to fix a sandwich. The news was on and I heard the news reporter talking about a shooting that took place at Paradise Kitty last night.

"This shit needs to stop. These niggas keep killing each other and then the mothers are on the news crying about their child wasn't in the street doing anything wrong. All of a sudden the muthafucka was a member of Fellowship Baptist church when in all honestly he was a member of one of the local gangs." I said out loud.

"Maximo Vasquez was one of the victims of last night's shootout. He died moments later at the hospital. Investigators doesn't have any suspects in custody. If anyone have any information about this horrific crime, contact 18th District police Department at (312) 555-1939. You don't have to disclose your identity when you call. In other news, there were six bodies discovered in the North Lawndale neighborhood. No suspects in that case and the victims has not been identified as of yet."

I had heard enough and turned the television off. The name Vasquez kept coming to mind and I stopped in my tracks. There were many Vasquez in this city, but Mauricio came to mind. He never told me his siblings names, I knew he had two brothers, though. Nah, that couldn't have been one of his brothers.

Going about my day, I cleaned up my apartment and did the few loads of laundry that needed to be done. In the middle of mopping the floor, Mauricio's name popped in my head again. I hadn't talked to him since the day I saw him on 79th street. Propping the mop against the wall, I went into my bedroom and grabbed my phone. I scrolled to Mauricio's name and pressed the button, he answered after the phone rang three times.

"What up, Miss Smith?" His voice was deep and sexy.

"I was calling to see how you were since I haven't talked to you."

"I'm making it. I'm in the middle of some shit right now, can I call you back when I'm done?"

"That's fine, but can I ask you something?"

"Sure, what is it?"

"Do you have a brother named Maximo?" I asked biting my finger nail.

"I had a brother name Maximo up until last night. We can talk about it when I hit you back, ma. I gotta go, I'll call you back," he said ending the call.

The feelings I was having couldn't be explained. I heard Mauricio trying to disguise the hurt in his voice. I didn't know what it was like to lose a loved one because I didn't have any. Shit I didn't even have a real damn family that I knew about.

Before I started the job as a correctional officer and finished college, I was a stripper. Life wasn't easy for me growing up at all. I'm lucky to have made it this far in life. But God had a plan for me and I was making the best of it. I was given a second chance at this thing called life.

My mama was a single parent that got involved with a guy that turned her into the neighborhood crackhead. At first, she was functioning and I didn't know she was dabbling with the booga suga. There was always food in the house and all the bills were paid. Then shit started going off without warning and her excuse was, " the company made a mistake."

One day I came home from school, I was fourteen years old. My mother was on the couch with her ass in the air and her boyfriend Dino was pounding into her from the back. I wasn't concentrating on the sexual act, what caught my eye was the needle that was sticking out of her arm while she snorted white powder into her nostrils.

"Mama, what are you doing?"

"Mind yo' business lil girl before I make you suck my dick!" he yelled at me.

Dino kept his eyes trained on me and I was scared to move a muscle. After a while I ran back out the door and didn't come back until later that night. When I entered our apartment, it was dark but I had an uneasy feeling in my stomach. Hitting the switch, the light flooded the room and my mama and Dino was laying on the couch with blood running from both of their heads.

I remember screaming until my throat was sore. The neighbors came knocking on the door and I couldn't open it right away. When I got up and opened the door, I was escorted out and the police was called. Out of all the mutha-fuckas that were around since I was little, none of them would take me in. Instead, I was hauled off to a fucking orphanage.

Didn't nobody want a teenager in their home. A couple months later I was placed in a home where an older woman named Paulette had five other kids in her custody. I learned early on that she didn't give a fuck about nothing but money. Her grown ass nephew was there to help with us but he was only there to get his dick wet with the little girls.

Tatiana was six years old, she was there because her mother took her to the police station when she was two weeks old and left her. Paulette had her since she was a month old. You would've thought she would treat her like more than a check. That wasn't the case though.

I woke up one night hearing Tati's muffled cries. Getting up out of my bed, I made my way down the hall following the sound. This nasty nigga had his mouth on that baby with his fingers in her little coochie. With all of the grown bitches out in the street willing to give it up for free, this bastard wanted to fuck with a baby.

"What the hell you doing?" I asked startling him.

"I—I was trying to see why her privates was hurting."

"Nigga, you think I'm stupid? I saw what you were doing to her!"

"You didn't see shit! Go the fuck to bed, Latorra. With yo' grown ass."

"Come on Tati," I said holding out my hand. She practically kicked him in his face to get off the couch. "You won't get away with this with yo' perverted ass."

He had his head down and I scooped the cordless phone up and called the police. When they arrived, he tried to deny everything. I had already told Tati it was okay to tell the police everything. He went to jail that night. Tati was taken out of the home and I was kicked out by Paulette because she said I was fucking up her money.

I didn't care, as long as I did what I had to do. I was in the orphanage until I was sixteen then I was placed in another home. I was the only kid in the household. It was the home of a preacher and his wife. What could happen in a preacher's home? Every damn thing.

I was beaten for tearing the toilet paper off the roll wrong. If I didn't like what was prepared for dinner, which was every day because the First Lady couldn't boil water,

I was beaten. On top of that, the pastor had a problem with his hands in other ways as well.

"Latorra, your body is just right for me," he said one day. "Let me massage your titties." He said wickedly.

"If you touch me, I'll bust yo' muthafuckin' head, dude."

His eyes grew to the size of golf balls and his face turned redder than a tomato. He lunged at me and grabbed me by my arms. He tried to kiss me and I kicked him in his dick. I would forever hear the loud howl he let fall from his throat. When he dropped to his knees, I kicked him in his face and ran out of the house. I've been on my own ever since.

The ringing of my phone brought me back to reality. I looked at the screen and it was my girl Tammy calling. "What's up, trick?" I said when I answered.

"Did you see all those damn shootings on the damn news? All of this shit makes my ass scared to go the fuck outside. I was supposed to be at Paradise Kitty last night, I didn't feel like partying after shaking my ass at Adrianna's. That fine ass nigga Mauricio had a birthday party and his brother was one of the people that died."

Tammy was the ghetto newscaster. She knew about everything that happened in the street better than channels two, five, seven, and nine. If I had been thinking clearly, I could've found out everything I wanted to know from her ass. She stayed on all that shit like it was her job to know.

"Do they know who did it?" I was trying to see if she had the inside scoop because the news didn't have access to that information.

"Word on the street is Floyd and his crew did it. Now them nigga's ain't nowhere to be found. Mauricio and nem clapped back because some of Floyd's workers got popped outside the trap on 16th Street. Clout was one of em. I'm pissed off because I'm gon' miss that nigga's dick!"

"Bitch really? Is that all you can say about that man and he's dead? So disrespectful. How do you know Mauricio had something to do with that? Don't be spreading rumors nah, Tammy."

"Girl bye, stop being so damn sensitive. He had a damn python between his legs. Who else did that shit? Anyway, I think it's about to be a lot more bodies laid out."

"Don't repeat that shit to nobody else. You don't even know if the people you putting at the scene did what you're implying. That's some dangerous shit." I tried to talk some sense into her ass, but she knew too much.

"You act like you know them niggas, yo' lame ass needs to get out so you can be up on the need to know. What you doing today? We should hang out."

I didn't want to hang out with Tammy. She was on a mission to get the scoop on the latest crimes like she was a detective or something. I wanted no parts of that. I had to deal with her messiness when we stripped together. Now that I didn't live that life anymore, our friendship wasn't quite the same.

"I'm not going out today. I will be staying in to get ready for work on Monday."

"Monday, Latorra, today is Saturday. If you don't want to hang out, say you don't want to hang out." She said with an attitude.

"Okay, Tammy, I don't want to go out. Is that better?"

"Fuck you then. Yo' ass changed." She said hanging up on me.

I didn't care if she was mad. I wasn't into the things she was into anymore. I changed for the better, something she should look into doing. Picking up the mop, I finished what

I had started and went to get my clothes out of the dryer. After hanging and folding most of my clothes I went to my room to take a nap.

I don't know how long I slept, but my phone ringing woke me. I snatched it up without checking to see who was calling. "Hello," I croaked out and cleared my throat.

"Were you sleep?" Mauricio asked quietly.

"Nah, I was watching tv."

"Yo' ass was sleep. I'll hit you back later. I said I'd call when I was done with business."

"No, it's okay. I'm awake."

"You lying but okay, hit me with yo' address. I want to take you out for dinner."

Looking at the time it was almost 6 o'clock. It didn't feel like I'd slept that damn long. "I don't know you like that to have you coming to my house."

"I'm not going through this with you tonight, Officer Smith. I want to spend time with you right now, don't deprive me of the chance to get to know you. Plus, you would be just what I need to get my mind off the shit I'm going through right now."

"Okay, I'll text you the address." I said.

"I'll be on my way as soon as you send the location," he said hanging up.

I sent him my address and I jumped up and ran to the bathroom. Showering quickly, I returned to my bedroom and oiled my body with shea butter. I really didn't want to go out so convincing Ricio to stay inside was what I had on my mind. I chose a pair of black leggings and a red tank top to put on. With everything that was going on, I didn't want someone to try to retaliate while he was with me. I might get hit by accident, I didn't want to take a chance.

As I waited for Mauricio to pull up, I put the last of my laundry away. He picked the right day to come through because usually during the week my place looked a mess. The hours I worked didn't permit me to keep things in order.

There was a knock on the door as I sat scrolling through my Facebook page. I looked at the time and it was six forty-five and I knew it was Mauricio. "Who is it?" I asked as I stood and walked to the door.

"Who you want it to be?" He asked from the other side.

His voice was so sexy to me and the tingle in my lower regimen was powerful. I wasn't trying to sleep with this man knowing that he had many women flocking to him. But the way my hormones were raging, that was something I'd have to keep preaching to myself. Opening the door, my breath caught in my throat and I couldn't find my voice.

This man had on a white and black Givenchy shirt, with a pair of black jeans of the same brand, and black and Givenchy sneakers to match. His hair was tapered on the sides and braided neatly on the top of his head. His beard was shaped and the way his goatee framed his lips had my eyes stuck.

"You gon' make a nigga stand outside until you get dressed?" he asked snapping me out of my trance.

"I'm sorry, come on in," I said stepping to the side. "I don't need to get dressed, I think we should order takeout instead."

I closed the door and led the way to the couch. Before I could walk past him, Mauricio grabbed me by the hand and brought my chest into his. The scent of his cologne was intoxicating . It was a struggle not to wrap my arms around his neck and plant a big kiss on his luscious lips.

"Tell me, why don't you want to go out for dinner?"

"I um—You are going through a lot right now with your family situation," I said looking away from him.

He turned my head back to face him and looked in my eyes. "I don't know what you have heard, but nothing will happen to you as long as you're with me. That is something I can promise you. Now, go in there and get dressed, you don't have to get all dolled up. We will go to Applebee's or somewhere like that."

"I don't know Mauricio. Do you know who did this to your brother?" I asked.

"Yeah, I do. That's not something you need to worry about, I got that handled. Trust me."

"How am I suppose to trust you when I don't even know anything about you?"

"That's the reason I want to take you out. I want to get to know you. To be honest, we can stay here and order something. I won't promise that I'd keep my hands to myself though." Mauricio smirked.

He slid his hand down to my ass and I reached back and moved his hand back to my waist. I wasn't expecting him to say what he did, nor did I think he would palm my ass, but my mind was on being manish too. The thing was, I was trying to prevent that action from taking place. It has been a minute since I just sexed a guy before getting to know him. Playing the field wasn't something I wanted to revert back to.

"That won't happen. I'm not one to get sexually aroused when I know I'm not giving up my goods. I'll be back in a few, make yourself at home," I said backing away from him.

I walked to the coffee table, handed him the remote and turned toward my bedroom. Putting an extra swing to my hips, I turned my head to see if he was still watching me.

He was and the way he licked his lips let me know if we stayed here, we would definitely end up fucking all over my apartment.

"Hurry yo' ass up, a nigga hungry," he said getting comfortable on the couch.

Rushing into my room, I scrambled through my closet trying to find something decent to put on. I decided on a black and pink sweat suit with my black Air Max sneakers. After tying my shoes, I looked in the mirror and saw a couple of strands of my hair was out of place. Quickly grabbing the brush, I smoothed my wrap back in place and slid some clear gloss across my lips.

I grabbed my purse, making sure I had my wallet and keys. I walked down the short hall to the living room and Mauricio's eyes were glued to the tv. He was watching the news with a scowl on his face. The segment was talking about the shooting at Paradise Kitty and the need for gun control in Chicago. The police superintendent was talking about bringing in the National Guard.

Mauricio's jaw was clenching tightly and his fists were opening and closing rapidly. There was a mixture of anger and hurt in his eyes. The murder of his brother was really hurting him but getting revenge was something he had to be thinking about strongly as well.

Once the segment was over, I took that moment to walk over and turned the tv off. His eyes were still focused on the screen and it seemed as if he was looking straight through me. The light bounced off his light brown pupils and a slight mist brimmed his lower lids.

"Mauricio, are you ready?" I asked softly.

Looking up at me, he lowered his head and nodded yes before letting out the breath he was apparently holding. He stood and his phone started ringing. Taking it from his hip, he looked at it and silenced it with a push of a button before walking to the door. I picked my phone up from the coffee table and followed him.

"Where are we going for dinner?"

"We can go where ever you want to go. All I want to do is spend a little time with yo' pretty ass," he said as I locked up.

"Chili's, let's go to Chili's. Chicken quesadillas sound pretty good right about now. Not to mention, I could go for a couple of margaritas too."

"Let's go then," he said grabbing my hand and leading the way to his black Benz.

Mauricio was quite the gentleman. He opened the passenger door for me, making sure I was comfortable before he closed the door. When he got in on the other side, he slid in smoothly and smiled at me. The dimple in his cheek was so cute. I looked away because my face heated up instantly. He started the car and the voice of 2Pac poured from the speakers.

How many brothers fell victim to the streets?
Rest in peace, young nigga, there's a heaven for a G
Be a lie if I told you that I never thought of death
My niggas, we the last ones left, but life goes on

Pushing the button on the steering wheel, Mauricio skipped the song to something more upbeat and happier. I could only imagine how many times he had listened to that track. We headed west on 79th street and I noticed how the neighborhood changed with every mile we drove. It went from abandoned buildings and liquor stores on every corner to nice houses and manicured lawns the closer we got to our destination.

"What's on your mind, Miss Smith?" Mauricio asked.

"I was thinking about how the neighborhoods in the hood are run down and all these neighborhoods are nice. If I had the funds, I would invest in our neighborhoods. It's sad how everything is today."

"Anyone can invest in these streets, but the niggas ain't gon' do nothing but tear it up all over again. The neighborhoods don't need to change, the people are what needs to change," he said shaking his head. "I'm in these streets doing what I do. I don't plan on being in the streets for the rest of my life, but I'm gon' do what I have to do before I leave it all alone," he said as he turned into the parking lot of the mall.

Mauricio pulled into a spot not far from the entrance and got out after turning the car off. He walked around to the passenger side and opened the door for me to get out. I had never had a man open and close a door for me in my life. I guess messing with good for nothing niggas was the reason why. Holding his hand out to help me out the car, I placed my hand in his and allowed him to lead the way into the mall.

We were seated right away and it wasn't too crowded for a Saturday evening. The waitress came over bringing water and menus for us to look over. I already knew what I had a taste for. Eating hadn't been on my mind until Mauricio called to take me out.

"Have you decided what you would like to eat, Miss Smith?"

"Mauricio, why do you always call me by my last name? It makes me feel like an old ass woman. Latorra would be fine from here on out."

"Okay, Latorra. What are you eating tonight?" he said with a sly grin.

"I will order once the waitress comes back. Do you know what you're going to eat?"

"Actually, I do. How have you been?" he asked taking a sip of water from his glass.

"I've been alright. Working long and hard at that damn prison. I'm glad I have the next couple of days off, I can get some much needed rest. The prisoners are something else. I couldn't imagine being locked up like an animal. Some of them are locked down twenty-three hours of the day. How do they expect them to act civilized if they are cooped up all damn day?"

"Miss Smith—I mean Latorra, being locked up is something I have never experienced a day in my life. Not even county lock up. The life they live, is something I would never know about. The judicial system is really fucked up and most of the cases are bullshit. There are many black men locked up for shit that another muthafucka of another race would get a slap on the wrist for. I'm not defending any crimes that have been committed because some are guilty as hell, but the amount of time given, ain't about shit. You need to go in there and do your job and go home. That's it that's all."

"I agree with the things you said and it's a shame. I don't socialize in that place because there's nothing behind the walls of a prison that excites me."

"What type of things do you like, Latorra? I'm asking for myself?" he said sipping more water.

"I like bowling, skating, going to poetry sets, movies, plays, reading, basically anything I can do and have fun doing it." I said taking a sip of water.

"You didn't mention clubbing. It's rare that a woman doesn't like to go out and shake her ass every once in a while," he laughed.

My mind was racing because I didn't know how much of my life, I wanted to share with him. Bringing up clubbing took me back to the days where clubbing was something, I did every weekend without hesitation. It also was the place that made me forget about all the shit I had been through.

"I don't club anymore, I work too much." Keeping it simple, I was glad the waitress finally decided to come take our order.

"Are you guys ready to order?" she said in her chipper voice.

"Actually, we are. I would like the chicken quesadillas and the boneless buffalo wings as an appetizer." I said placing my order.

"Would you like salad or fries with that ma'am?"

"I will take fries, thank you."

"Okay. what would you like, sir?"

"I would like to have the Classic sirloin with the loaded mashed potatoes and steamed broccoli topped with cheese. I would also like a half rack of ribs and a margarita and a strawberry lemonade."

"Okay, I will put your order in and your appetizers will be out soon. Thank you for choosing Chili's." She said as she collected the menus and walked away.

Staring at Mauricio across the table, I took in all of his features and was able to see just how handsome he really was. He looked like he hadn't been to sleep all night. The coloring under his eyes could be seen in the light above the table and the events of the night before came to mind. I didn't know exactly what happened, but I wanted to know how he was really dealing with what took place.

"Mauricio, can I ask you a question?"

"Yeah, what's on your mind, ma?"

"I want you to tell me how you're really doing. You don't have to tell me that you're alright because I know you're not. Tell me the truth, Mauricio."

"Losing my baby brother is something I never expected. This has opened the wound from when my parents were killed. I won't sit here and say I don't have revenge on my mind because I do. You don't have to worry about any of that though. Enough about me, tell me about your life before being a correctional officer."

I was sipping on my water when he made that last statement, I started coughing uncontrollably because it went down the wrong pipe. Mauricio got up and sat next to me patting my back. Tears were running down my face and I was glad I didn't have on any makeup. I was finally able to stop coughing and took another sip of water.

"You good?" he asked with concern in his voice.

"Yes, I'm alright, the water went down wrong."

"So, are you ready to tell me about Latorra?"

"There's not much to tell. I was raised in foster care after my mama died and I don't know my father. I moved from foster home to foster home until I was sixteen and have been on my own since. I don't have any kids, end of story."

He chuckled and looked over at me, "there is a back story in there somewhere. I won't pressure you to disclose whatever it is until you're ready. Until then, I would love to spend time with you. I will be kind of busy but I will put forth the effort to call and stop by if that's okay with you."

"That would be fine, I'd like that. Here comes our food, you may want to go back to the other side of the table because I'm going to need all this space to smash this food." I said jokingly.

"I'm with you on that, I'm about to fuck some shit up too."

We both laughed as the waitress sat the food on the table along with the drinks. Once everything was placed, he got up and slid in the booth on the other side. Silently eating our food, I thought about how I was really starting to like Mauricio as more than a friend. I have never had a man hear the version of my life that I wanted to expose and leave it up to me to tell him more about it.

"What are you over there thinking about, ma? Your mind is somewhere else."

Looking up with a smile, I bit into a quesadilla so I wouldn't have to disclose my thoughts right away. After, I took a long sip of the margarita and sat the glass down. "I was thinking about how I would like to get to know you as well, Mr. Vasquez. You're a smooth talker but I think I'll give you a chance to show me what you have in store for me."

"The first thing I want to do is clean your damn mouth before somebody thinks you been doing something other than eating," he laughed as he wiped the side of my mouth with a napkin.

"Shut up and thanks with your nasty ass." I said blushing like a school girl.

He leaned over the table and I did the same. His lips were almost on mine when a voice interrupted the moment. "Hey, Ricio. Where's Nija while you're out here entertaining the next bitch?"

I looked up and there stood a beautiful woman with her hand on her hip with two other women standing next to her. She was glancing back and forth between the two of us making me remember he had a tribe of females all over the city. Picking up my glass, I waited for him to address the woman because I was going to let the bitch word slide for the moment.

"Nihiyah, I don't know where she is. Watch your mouth, you have no reason to call her out her name. If she knocks your fuckin' teeth out of your head, she would have every right to do that shit. Now, get the fuck away from me. Go find a dick or two to ride." He said picking his fork up. "Sorry about—"

"I don't need to respect this bitch! You think because you run around this muthafucka killing people, I'm supposed to be scared of you! Fuck you!"

"Keep yo' damn voice down! Whatever the fuck I do ain't yo' concern. Wherever you getting' yo information from, tell them mufuckas to get the shit right. It's not in your best interest to spread rumors you don't know shit about, Nihiyah. On the strength of yo' mama and Nija is the reason yo' ass ain't laid out in this bitch. For the last time, get the fuck away from me!" The vein in his temple protruded out and his face hardened with every word he spoke. "Don't worry about it," he said throwing money on the table. "Let's go."

Mauricio stood and held his hand out to help me out of the booth. Nihiyah or whatever her name was, followed us out with her two bodyguards right behind her. I had a feeling something was about to happen but I didn't know what. All I wanted to do was make it to the car without an altercation. But she wouldn't leave well enough alone.

"You threatening to put your hands on me, don't mean shit, Ricio! Yo' punk ass ain't shit without a gun, nigga. What happened to yo' brother could easily happen to yo' pussy ass!" she yelled as she pushed him in the back of his head.

Before I could stop him, Mauricio spun around and in one long stride grabbed her by her throat. "Bitch, if you ever mention my brother again, I will kill yo' hoe ass! Stay outta my business! As far as anybody comin' for me, tell them to get their army ready!" he snarled as he shoved her to the ground.

"Oh, you put yo' hands on the wrong one, Ricio! Watch ya'self, nigga. I don't care how much my sister loves yo' ass, you done fucked up!" she yelled as she punched buttons on her phone.

Mauricio went after her again and I grabbed him by the arm, "she's not worth it, let's go." I said in a shaky voice. I didn't want him to go to jail for beating her ass. He allowed me to lead him to the car and once we were inside, I kept my eye on the Nihiyah girl. Her lips were moving as she talked to whomever she had on the phone and her head was whipping around rapidly. She looked up and threw her middle finger in the air as we drove off.

"I hope you don't let that bullshit get in your head. She is one messy bitch and there's a lot of suspicion with the shit she pulled tonight. That didn't have shit to do with her seeing me with you. It's deeper than that. I'm dropping you off at home, I have some shit to figure out. Sorry to cut our night short, ma. I'll make it up to you." He said as we headed back to my house.

Chapter 8
Sincere

After leaving the warehouse, Beast and the guys went to the storage facility to bring the product back. The cleanup crew was there to get the warehouse ready for operation. There would be safes installed in the walls and other things that were needed in order for things to run smoothly with what was in store.

I was on my way to the hospital to check on Madysen. I stopped at the mall to get her an outfit to wear home because she wouldn't be able to put the clothes on from last night. When I saw her the night before she looked as if she was going to die right along with Max. I felt sorry for the poor girl, I needed to talk to her to see if there was anything she knew that would shed some light on what was going on with him.

I needed to get to the bottom of what was eating him from the inside. Max was a very good kid that was forced to live the life he'd lived. Big Jim was the last person that needed to have custody of those kids. I never liked him from the first day I met him. There was always something off about him, but he kept the shit hidden well. He was on the top of my list of people to get at.

Sosa on the other hand was going out of his fuckin' mind, I like that shit though. The way Rodrigo laid down the law was the shit that had me cheering inside. Anyone that could stand up to my man without being disrespectful, was *that nigga* to me. My nephew was about to be a force to be reckoned with. Personally, I was going to try my best to keep an eye on him because he was liable to kill everyone before I had a chance.

My stomach was rumbling and I was hungry as hell. I would grab something to eat after I finished with Madysen. Easing in a spot a short distance away from the entrance, I turned the car off and got out. There was a group of people standing outside crying. The scene before me reminded me of the way my family was gathered outside this very hospital the night before. There will be many more sheds of tears shed before all is said and done.

After getting a pass at the counter, I went to the elevator heading for the third floor. The doors opened and one of Floyd's flunkies got off the elevator talking on his phone. As he passed me, I caught part of his conversation and I wanted to follow him and put a slug in the back of his head.

"Man, I can't believe them niggas got to Clout. I'm killing them niggas in broad daylight if that's when I see 'em."

Deciding to let him live a bit longer, I got on the elevator and pressed the number three and laid my head back. I remembered the name Clout from the meeting and shit was about to heat up quickly. I pulled my phone from my purse and sent Beast a text.

Sin: Tell everybody to stay on alert. I just saw one of the opps at the hospital. They are looking to retaliate for the shit on 16th whenever and where ever. We need to be on the same shit!"

The doors to the elevator opened and I stepped off looking for room 312. When I found it, I knocked softly on the door. Madysen didn't respond so I took the liberty of walking in without permission. The tv was on low and she was lying on her side with her back to the door. I walked to the other side of the bed to see if she was asleep.

She was sleeping soundly so, I sat down in the chair and looked down at my phone. Beast had replied to my text. I opened it and read what he had to say.

Beast: I let them know what's up. I want you to be careful, Sin. Don't be out there trying to handle shit by yourself. I'm not worried about them niggas coming for you because they don't know nothing about you. I want to keep it that way.

I don't know why he thought I was going to sit back and let this shit play out. I knew about the trap on 16th street and the one on 26th, they won't let me in on any of the other spots but I wasn't going to let that bother me. There were many ways to find out shit and I was determined to get the information I needed.

Sin: I hear you Erique.

"Sin," I looked over at Madysen after I heard her say my name. "Please tell me I was dreaming about Max dying."

Lying my phone on the food tray that sat beside the bed, I grabbed her hand. She was shaking slightly and I didn't want to upset her but there was no reason to give her false hope. The only thing I could do was be straight up with her.

"No baby, it wasn't a dream. Everything will be alright, Madysen."

"It's not going to be alright, Sin! How am I supposed to live without him? I would rather be dead too, he was all I had!" she cried snatching away from me.

"Madysen, I need you to calm down. Talking like that is the reason you are in this part of the hospital. If you keep it up, they are gonna ship yo' ass to the mental hospital and lock you up until they feel the need to let you out. I know you're not crazy, but they don't. What happened to Max was fucked up and I wish he was still here. But he's not."

"I don't want to live anymore, Sin."

"Say that shit again and I will slap the snot outta yo ass! You are too young to think your life is over because Max

83

isn't here! You were apart of this family and you will continue to be. Do you think we would turn our backs on you like that?" I waited for her to respond and when she didn't, it pissed me off more. "Do you?" I asked standing over her.

Shaking her head back and forth, I sat down in the chair. After listening to her cry for the next ten minutes I'd enough. I snatched a couple pieces of tissue out of the pack and handed them to her.

"Listen to me. We are all hurting over the loss of Max. He was the baby of the family and he didn't deserve that shit. I need for you to get your head together, that's the only way you can get out of this muthafucka." I said calmly. Before I could continue, there was a light tap on the door and the doctor walked in.

"Hello, I'm Dr. Langstein and you must be Madysen," he said closing the door behind him. "Who may you be?" he said directing his attention to me.

"I'm her aunt Sincere, nice to meet you. How is she?" I asked.

"Madysen hasn't really been talking to us today but I think she is progressing fine. With everything that she witnessed, the sedative has worn off but she seems to be very depressed. Only time can heal her from that and it's understandable why she is feeling the way that she is. I came in to deliver Miss Wright some good news. Hopefully it will brighten her day," he said with a smile.

"The only news I want to hear is you telling me I can go home. Other than that, I don't want to hear nothing else." Madysen shot back at him.

"Miss Wright, I think what I have to say is just as exciting as you going home."

Madysen was giving this doctor so much attitude and it was hard for me not to hold in the laughter I wanted to let out. The expression on his face had him looking like a puppet waiting for his strings to be pulled on what to do next. He was twirling the clipboard in his hands nervously.

"Well, your lab work came back and I want to say, congratulations! You're having a baby!"

Both Madysen and I sat staring at him as if he had two heads. That was the last thing I expected him to say out of his mouth. My focus went to Madysen and tears were falling down her cheeks. She fell back on the pillows and covered her face with her hands.

"Are you sure?" she asked in between sobs.

"The results from both your urine and blood samples read the same, positive. I hope those are happy tears, Miss Wright. Children are blessings," Dr. Langstein said smiling. "I scheduled you for an ultrasound, the sonographer will be coming in any minute."

He didn't fully finish what he was saying before there was a knock on the door. A young woman in purple scrubs rolled the ultrasound machine into the room bearing a wide grin. It was evident that she loved her job.

"Who's ready to see how this beautiful bundle is baking inside the mommy to be?" When Madysen didn't respond, she frowned briefly but forced a smile quickly. "My name is Leslie, I will be the one to show you the first images of your little peanut," she said as she plugged in the machine. Placing a tube in a warming container, she looked over at us. "I'm warming up the gel before I apply it to your stomach, it can be very cold if I don't do this."

Madysen wasn't the least bit enthused about this process. She looked like she was mad at the world, on top of being sad at the same time. I was worried about her mental state at first, now I was *really* worried. Leslie folded back the sheet that covered Madysen and lifted her gown exposing her stomach.

It was the first time I noticed any signs of pregnancy because she was big boned and always had a slight pudge. At closer glance, she was definitely pregnant. There was no way Madysen didn't know this until now.

Leslie applied the gel on Madysen's stomach and grabbed a wand like object. She moved it around as she looked at the screen. Instantly the sound of the baby's heartbeat filled the room. Dr. Langstein moved closer to the screen and both he and Leslie were staring at it intensely. Curiosity was eating me up inside and I wanted to see what they were seeing.

I rose from the chair I was sitting in as Dr. Langstein spoke out loud. "Miss Wright, when was your last menstrual cycle?"

"Last week. It was on time and lasted five days. I've had a period every month as usual, that's how I know for a fact I'm not pregnant," she said with her eyes closed.

"What you have been experiencing is something that is simply called vaginal bleeding. It's usually a watery like substance unlike your regular cycle. Do you experience any cramping along with the bleeding?" he asked without taking his eyes off the monitor.

"The cramping is not more than the usual cramping that comes when I'm on my period. It lasts maybe, a couple hours or so." Madysen replied.

I stood up and walked behind Leslies chair and damn near choked on nothing. What I was witnessing was a full fledge baby on the screen sucking its thumb. There were eyes, nose, fingers, toes, the whole nine yards. Madysen was pregnant pregnant and she didn't look like it at all. She had to be carrying this baby in all those titties and ass that she had.

"How far along is she in this pregnancy?" I asked out loud.

Leslie moved the wand and pressed a couple buttons in between movements. This lasted a couple minutes before a series of numbers appeared on the bottom of the screen. "According to the measurements, and the development of the baby, I would say that you are approximately twenty-seven to thirty weeks pregnant, Madysen."

Doing the calculations in my head, I turned quickly to the bed Madysen was lying in. "Seven months, Madysen! You can't sit here and tell me you didn't know about this!"

"I didn't know! I had suspicions that I was and I even told Max—" she paused after saying his name and the tears started again. I sat on the edge of the bed and wrapped her in my arms. "I told him about it and he bought several tests and they all were negative so I didn't think anymore about it. My period came every month like clockwork. The only thing that changed was my breasts and butt. I'm a little heavier than usual but I've always been thick as hell."

"Okay, don't cry. Everything will be alright. That's a baby in there, somewhere," I laughed. "There's nothing we can do about it now but wait until it arrives. Can you tell what the sex is, Leslie?" I asked excitedly.

Seeing the baby had me happier than a nun in a room full of dicks. I wasn't able to conceive any children due to something that happened to me in the past. I've always wanted to be a mother, but being an aunt isn't too bad, I'd take it. Leslie was back to tapping away on the keys with one hand, while moving the wand with the other. Her eyes lit up and she smiled brightly clicking the mouse.

"We got a boy! Lawd, lil man is gon' be blessed!" she laughed.

"Leslie! That was not the appropriate thing to say!" Dr. Langstein said scolding her.

"I'm sorry, Dr. Langstein. Would you all like to have the sonograms in 3D?"

"Lighten up doc, it's okay. Leslie is only telling it like it is," I laughed. "Yes, Leslie. As well as the originals."

She printed out the copies and started packing up the equipment. Pushing the machine toward the door, Leslie stopped by the bed and wiped Madysen's stomach with a paper towel and covered her up. "Congratulations, Madysen."

"Thanks," she said without feeling.

"Congratulations, Miss Wright. I will get your discharge papers together and I will also set up your first appointment with an obstetrician that I trust with my life. Dr. Cheryl Langstein is my wife and she will take very good care of you. Plus, I want to be around when this little one enters the world. I want you to get the prescription for the prenatal vitamins as soon as possible. You have gone seven months without any prenatal care and I'm glad everything looks good with the baby. We are going to make the last two months count, I'll be back in the next thirty minutes. Sit tight," he said before leaving the room.

Madysen automatically turned her back to me. I refused to let her shut me out. We was going to talk about how she was feeling. The way she was acting told me she was not happy about the baby. I believed if Max was still here with us, she would be ecstatic about the situation.

"Come on Mads, this is an exciting occasion, sweetie. Max wouldn't want you to be sad. You have to pull yourself together because the baby feeds off your energy."

"There's no way I can support a baby! I'm twenty years old and Max paid for everything. He wanted me to concentrate on school and didn't want me to work. The money I do have in my account isn't nearly enough to take care of this baby, Sin. Max was all I had. He was my family."

"First of all, you don't let nan nigga tell you not to work. Yes, you are in school and that's great. Never depend on another muthafucka to secure your bag for you. I'm not clowning you by any means, but having your own puts that security in place just in case that nigga wants to leave. Max didn't have a say in the reason he is no longer here. If you had paved your own way financially, trying to make it wouldn't be a concern. I don't know what you've been through, but I do know you won't struggle a day with this baby as long as Max's blood runs through his veins," I had to school her young ass for a minute. Madysen had my full support, no matter what. She didn't understand how much life she has given back to this family.

"I don't know, Sin. I don't want this baby! I don't even want to live! I've lost the love of my life and I don't think I will be able to go on without him." she cried out.

"Stop right now! You are not your only concern anymore. There is a life inside of you and he needs you in order to enter this world healthy. You sound selfish as fuck right now, Madysen! I know you are hurt that Max died, we all are. His death is affecting everybody that loved him, not just you! Listen to me," I said calming myself down. "I will talk to Beast. You can stay with us until shit blows over in the streets. Going back to your apartment is not an option as long as Floyd and his crew are out and about. What I want you to do is get your mind right to say your final goodbyes to Max. Can you do that for me? Do it for your son, he needs you, Madysen."

Silently crying, she nodded her head yes. I knew she didn't mean that shit, that's why I had to keep an eye on her ass. In my mind I knew I was going to have to beat her ass. There was a light knock on the door and Dr. Langstein entered.

"Okay, Miss Wright you are all set to get out of here. I set up your OB-GYN appointment and these are the prescriptions for your prenatal pills. Take care of yourself, Madysen." He said as he handed her the papers.

"Thank you," she said putting the papers on the night stand.

Dr. Langstein left the room and Madysen sat up in the bed. She stared straight ahead for a few minutes before she got up and went to the closet. She fell to her knees clutching the clothes that were in a plastic bag in her hands. Her gut wrenching sobs tugged at my heart.

"I have fresh clothes for you to put on, Madysen. Give me the bag." Taking the bag from her grasp, I walked to the other side of the room. I grabbed the bag with the clothes I'd bought and gave it to her.

"I'm not gonna be able to make it through this, Sin." She cried.

"Yes, you are and you will. I need you to go in the bathroom and get dressed," I said while helping her to her feet. Ushering her into the bathroom, I pressed the call button on the remote. A nurse came into the room a few minutes later.

"You need help, Miss Wright?" she asked when she stepped inside the room.

"Yes, I do. Can you please do me a favor and throw these clothes away for me?"

"Sure, I'm sorry, we didn't want to get rid of them without permission."

"It's okay and thank you."

"You're welcome. Is there anything else I can help you with?"

"No, you all have done plenty."

She left out the room with the bloodied clothes and I pulled my phone from my purse. I started a text to Beast then decided to call him instead. The phone rang and I waited for him to answer. His deep baritone was the calm that I need at the moment and I welcomed it.

"Hey babe, how's Madysen?"

"She's pregnant, Beast. I'm two seconds from knocking her upside her head because she's talking crazy as fuck. The only reason I'm keeping my cool is because I know she's grieving for Max. It goes beyond that though, I really believe she doesn't want to live without him."

"Bring her to the house, Sin. She can't go back to that apartment. We have to be sure to keep her happy and putting your hands on her is not gon' solve anything. We have to convince her to keep this baby, Sin."

"She doesn't have a choice in the matter, she's seven fuckin' months! The baby is coming if she wants it or not. Beast, she is talking as if she's going to do something to herself. If she does, she bet not make it because I'm killing her ass the first chance I get."

"She's not gon' do nothing to harm that damn baby, calm yo' trigga happy ass down! Take her to the house and get her settled in one of the guest rooms. Don't let her out of your sight, Sin. I will be there some time this evening and I will go to her place personally to get her shit."

"Do I look like a muthafuckin' babysitter? I have a funeral to plan and I'm supposed to meet Nija at her house to go over everything."

"Tell Nija to come to the house. Do as I say, Sin. I have to go, consider her feelings when you're talking to her. I know you are all hardcore and shit, put it to the side for now. I need you to be there for her, she needs that motherly love right now."

"I'm not her fuck—"

"I didn't ask you who you were, I already stated what I needed you to do, I'm looking for you to follow through with it. End of discussion. I love you, Sincere," he said cutting me off.

"Fuck you, Beast," was my response before I hung up on his ass. I didn't know who the fuck he thought he was talking to, but he knew I didn't take orders from no muthafucka.

Madysen came out of the bathroom wearing the Nike jogging suit and sneakers I purchased for her. I had already gathered all of the papers and put them in my purse. She glanced around the room and grabbed her phone from the night stand.

"I'm ready." She said heading for the door. I followed her while texting Nija to meet me at the house in about an hour. Mentally getting my mind together, I waited for the elevators doors to open while Madysen rested her head on the wall.

Chapter 9
Nija

I hadn't heard from Ricio since he left to go take care of business earlier this morning. After taking care of my hygiene, I put on a pair of jeans and a red off the shoulder 'Damn Right I'm From Chicago' shirt I'd bought online from Felicity Designs. It was time for me to go see my mama because it's been a while since I've seen her. She was the person I sought out when I needed to clear my head.

Leaving Ricio's condo, I went to the elevator and made my way to the garage. I hit the button to unlock the doors and jumped in. Picking my phone up I called my mom to see if she would be home before I showed up and she wasn't there.

"Hey, Nija baby! How have you been?"

"I'm doing well, ma. I'm on my way to your house, are you there?" I asked putting the car in drive.

"Yes, I'm here. I'm taking this big pan of lasagna out of the oven. Come on over and I will make sure I have things ready so we can sit down and talk about whatever you need to talk about, baby."

"That sounds so good! I am on my way as we speak."

"Nija I know damn well you're not talking on the phone and driving! What have I told you about that? Get off that phone now!"

"Calm down, ma. I haven't even pulled out of the garage," I said laughing.

"Garage? You must be at Mauricio's house. How's he doing anyway? Nihiyah told me about Max. That poor family just can't get a break." I could see her now, leaning against the counter with her head down sending a silent prayer up for the family.

"I'll talk to you about it when I get there. For now, I have to get off this phone before my mama whoop me," I said jokingly.

"As long as you know I will still knock you upside the head, no matter how old you get. That sister of yours on the other hand is going to make me shoot her ass between the eyes with her disrespectful ass."

Nihiyah was a subject I wasn't in the mood to discuss. I knew my mama was going to tell me everything that had been going on between the two of them. One thing I knew was she better not let it slip that Nihiyah put her hands on her.

"Save that for when I get there, ma. I'm on my way." I said preparing to end the call.

"Okay, baby. Drive safely and lock your doors. Love you."

"Love you too, ma. See you in a minute."

Ending the call, I threw my phone in the cup holder and pulled out of the garage. As I hopped on the expressway, traffic was light and I would be on the Southside in no time. Queen Naija's *Medicine* was playing on the radio. Turning it up, I soaked in the lyrics and Ricio came to mind. My phone rang before I could get deep in thought and I was happy about that shit.

"Hello," I said after putting the call on speaker without looking to see who was calling.

"Hey sis! How you doing over there? I heard about Max, why didn't you call me?"

My girl Kimmie was one of the only females I fucked with heavily when I wasn't with Ricio's ass. We'd been friends since elementary school and I loved her with everything in me. Kimmie didn't agree with the relationship I had with Ricio because she felt he was stringing me along. The thing about it though, she never ridiculed me about it but, she was always there when I needed her.

"It happened so fast, Kimmie. I wasn't thinking about calling anyone at the time. Seeing Max lying outside of the club riddled with bullets was something I never imagined witnessing. Then to get to the hospital and hearing the words he didn't make it, tore my heart to shreds. You of all people know that's my family."

"It sounds like you're driving. We need to catch up, where are you headed?"

"Yeah, I'm driving. I'm on my way to mama's house, she cooked lasagna and I'm going to smash. Yes, we do need to catch up. There's so much I have to fill you in on."

"Okay, bet. Call me when you're ten minutes away, I'll meet you over there. I need some of mama's food in my life."

"Mama would love to see you too."

"Girl bye! I've seen mama Pat more than your ass in the past week," she said laughing.

"Let me find out you trying to take my mama from me," I laughed. "I'm on the expressway passing 55th now. I should be in your neck of the woods shortly. You are only down the street from mama's house. Don't meet me there, beat me there, bitch,"

I hung up because I knew Kimmie was going to try saying something slick if I didn't. She was going to be petty as hell when she pulled up on me. While driving, I thought about how I put my foot in my mouth when I volunteered to plan Max's funeral. Sin was helping out but I still didn't think I would be able to get through it. The sound of

Madysen's high pitched wail after Max fell to the ground would forever be in my mind to remind me of that night.

The story of Max and Butta's murders were on every news station. I was waiting on one of the reporters to say there was a suspect in custody. Of course, that wasn't going to happen because the police weren't looking for any suspects. With all the cameras placed around the city, the Chicago Police Department won't pull the footage to see what happened. Let one of their own get gunned down, they would have someone locked up within twenty-four hours of the incident.

A lonely tear escaped from my eye and I wiped it away quickly. Last night I cried more than I ever had in my life. The hurt I felt was worse than the day I cried when my daddy left us for his other family. Ricio worked my body and temporarily took the pain away.

As I neared my mama's house, I noticed Nihiyah's car parked in the driveway. Dealing with her attitude was something I didn't want to endure that day. She always seemed to have a chip on her shoulder. For her sake, she better not come with any bullshit because I wasn't for it at all.

I parked on the street because for whatever reason my mom didn't park in the garage. When I got out of my car, Kimmie was parking on the other side of the street. She stared at me like she wanted to snipe my ass but I couldn't do anything but laugh at her. Kimmie jumped out of her car and I knew she was about to be on one.

"Bitch, I will beat yo' ass if you ever hang up on me again!"

"You ain't gon' bust a grape. Get yo' ass outta here with that tough cookie ass shit." I said embracing her in a hug.

"You are lucky I love yo' ugly ass." she said hugging me back. "You didn't sleep very well last night, I see."

"Nah, not really. Every time I closed my eyes the scene from the club was front and center. I agreed to help plan Max's funeral, now I don't know if I can do it."

"Nija you can and you will. I'm here to help any way that I can. All you have to do is tell me what you need me to do."

"Can you go on Max's social media pages and collect any pictures that he has so I can put them in the obituary? I doubt if he has any of him and Madysen, but check anyway. Speaking of Madysen, I have to call and see how she's doing. Kimmie, I'm glad you weren't able to come to the party."

"If I was there, I would've been busting my new nine right along with them niggas. Who did this shit, Nija?"

"It was Floyd and his crew. That's between us though, it doesn't go no further than here."

"Who the hell you think you're talking to, Nija? That's something we don't do. What we talk about stays between us. I've never gone behind your back repeating shit we talk about." she rolled her eyes.

"Look, I have to say that shit. You know I trust you with my life but I don't want anyone to know that you know anything about what's going on. It's about to get messy out here and I don't want you to be in the middle of the gunfight."

"Trust ain't a problem when it comes to me and you. With the information you just laid on me, your sister is the one you need to keep your eyes open for. I know Nihiyah is your sister but—"

"Are y'all gonna stand out there running ya mouths for the rest of the night? Get in here so I can eat!" my mama yelled from the front door before Kimmie could finish what she was about to say.

"Okay, mama Pat, we're coming right now." Kimmie hollered back. "Come on, I'll fill you in later," she said as we walked toward the house.

The aroma of fresh garlic bread hit me as I walked through the door. My stomach grumbled loudly because I hadn't eaten all day. Walking in to the dining room, the table was set for three and mama walked out the kitchen carrying dinnerware for Kimmie.

"Kimmie why didn't you call to let me know you were coming over?" mama asked as she set everything on the table.

"I just found out you were cooking when Nija told me she was on her way here. You know I love you though, mama." Kimmie said hugging her from behind.

"She's not your mama. The last time I checked she only had two kids." Nihiyah said walking from the back of the house.

"Don't start that shit tonight, Hiyah," my mama warned.

"Whatevver."

Nihiyah glared at us as she sat at the table. She was typing away on her phone intently and I was glad she found something to occupy herself before she got slapped. Nihiyah had always been jealous of the bond that Kimmie had with my mama. Mama took Kimmie in when her mom passed away and Nihiyah felt Kimmie got more love than she did, which was not the case. If Nihiyah had stayed out the streets she would've been there to get the love she craved from my mama.

Kimmie ignored her comment and we went into the kitchen to wash our hands. I could feel my mama's presence before she opened her mouth. "How many times do I have to tell y'all not to wash your hands in my sink? That's what the bathroom is for, don't let it happen again."

"We've been doing that for years and you still haven't reprimanded us for it. So, why stop now?" I laughed.

"Make me fuck you up, Nija. Don't play with me. Grab a pan and take it to the table. Kimmie grab the mats and the pitcher of sweet tea, don't come back into my kitchen until it's time for the both of you to wash the dishes." She said grabbing the bowl of garlic bread as well as the bowl of sweet peas.

We laughed as we grabbed the items and went back to the dining room. Nihiyah was still tapping on her phone with her head down. As mama sat the bread on the table, she reached to grab a piece and mama slapped her hand down.

"Don't put your nasty hands in my food! Go wash your hands, Hiyah."

"I washed my hands before I came out of the bathroom. I'm not a kid, don't put yo' hands on me no mo'." She sneered.

"Who the fuck you think you're talking to like that, Hiyah? If you were so grown you wouldn't be coming to my house every damn day to eat. Grown motherfuckers have jobs, where is yours?" my mama shot back at her. "I'd advise you to watch the words that come out your mouth when you're talking to me. I'm tired of your disrespectful ass."

Nihiyah was looking at her like a horn had grown out the middle of her forehead. After a couple minutes she got up and went to wash her hands. My sister was twenty-three years old and she didn't have any goals set for her life. She lived off my mama, expecting to get taken care of like she was still a child. With all the niggas she fucked with, you would think she would be able to take care of herself.

That wasn't the case, she got very angry when mama told her no. Whenever Nihiyah didn't get her way she found a way to start an argument. She needed to respect my mama or I was the one that was going to bust her shit.

We all fixed our plates and sat down to eat. The lasagna smelled good and it was cheesy as hell. I took a bite and looked across the table and gave my mama a thumbs up. She started laughing because she knew I loved lasagna.

"So, tell me what happened to Max. It's been repeatedly talked about on the news but they're not giving any major details," mom said taking a sip of her tea.

Nihiyah came back to the table and started fixing her plate. I was about to answer my mom when she opened her mouth letting stupid shit come out of it. "If he wouldn't have tried to be a hero, he would still be alive." She mumbled under her breath.

"What was that, Hiyah? Mom asked.

"Nihiyah, you weren't even there. Wasn't nobody trying to be a hero, whoever was shooting is ignorant as hell. You sound stupid as fuck repeating that crap," I snapped.

"Nija, yo' gullible ass don't even know what's going on around you. I think you need to stay away from Ricio before you end up in a box. You were almost there when his truck got shot up on 79th," she said cockily.

"Wait a damn minute, when did this happen?" my mama asked letting her fork fall into her plate.

I wanted to slap the fuck out of Nihiyah because now my mama was going to be worried about me. Nihiyah sat eating without looking up, she knew she had just started some shit. I'd kept that incident from my mother for that reason alone, but obviously Nihiyah knew I hadn't said anything to her about it.

"Earlier this week we were coming from the restaurant and some fools were shooting. We just so happened to driving down the street they were shooting on. They were not shooting at Ricio." I said trying to downplay the situation.

"That's not the way I heard it. Two people were killed that day and word on the street is Ricio did it. You can keep on believing the lies he's telling if you want to. His truck gets shot up, then his brother gets shot days later. Open your eyes Nija. While you're shackin' up with his ass, do you know where he was earlier?" she asked with a sly grin on her face. Not giving me a chance to respond, she continued. "With another bitch, that's where. If I hadn't approached his ass, he would've had his tongue down her throat."

"Hiyah, Ricio is free to do whatever he wants to do, he's not my man. I don't have to shack up with anyone because I have my own spot where I pay the bills, all by my lonesome. You should try it sometime, you may like it. Maybe then you could get the hell out of mama's house. I don't know what your problem is, but there's nothing you can say to upset me. Right now, you're acting like one of these young, jealous females out in the street. Getting mad about something a nigga is doing is what you do, I don't have time for any of that. Another thing, don't make assumptions about some shit you know nothing about, okay?"

"Hold up a minute. I want both of you to cut this mess out now! Nija and Nihiyah, watch ya mouths in my house."

My mama was getting frustrated and I could tell, but her daughter was saying things that could get her killed. If Nihiyah was running off at the mouth to us, who knew what she was saying to whomever would listen in the streets. How did she know about the shooting that day? I wondered to myself.

"I'm sorry for cussing but your daughter is skating on thin ice. Nihiyah, where are you getting your information? We don't know anything about the shooting and we were there. For you not to even be at the party that night, how do you know so much?"

"Don't worry about all that, little sister. Just know, Ricio is gonna get what's coming to him. He needs to realize that he is not his daddy, but he will end up just like him real soon." Nihiyah said putting a small chunk of lasagna in her mouth.

"I know this don't have anything to do with me—" Kimmie was saying before she was rudely cut off.

"You got that shit right. I don't even know why you are always in my damn house!" Nihiyah said pointing her fork at Kimmie.

"Mama Pat, I apologize in advance. Nihiyah let me tell you something, I have never done anything for you to dislike me the way you do. It never seems to be a problem when you see me outside of this house and you're asking me for money. But lately I've been telling you no so now you hate me. Since you have a lot of tea to spill, did you tell your mama that you fell in love with snow?"

"That ain't your business, bitch!" Nihiyah yelled jumping to her feet.

"There's no snow outside, Kimmie. What are you talking about?"

"She's not talking about nothing mama! Bitch you better shut yo' muthafuckin' mouth right now!"

Nihiyah walked around the table and Kimmie and I jumped up. "Nihiyah, calm down," I said stepping in her path.

"Move out of my way, Nija! This bitch is running her dick suckas and I'm about to close her shit!"

Nihiyah kept trying to get around me, but I wouldn't let her pass. "Get the fuck out of my way, Nija!"

"Now, you want to fight because you in here trying to pop off and the tables turned on you! If you want to reveal some shit, reveal what you got going on, Nihiyah. Admit it, you have a cocaine problem. Your secret is out, what you gon' do now?" Kimmie said not backing down from the daggers my sister shot at her.

"Is this true, Hiyah?"

"Hell nawl it's not true! This bitch lying and I'm about to fuck her up!" Nihiyah pushed me and I had to stand strong in order to prevent her from passing me. They weren't about to tear up my mama's house. Nihiyah looked like a pitbull foaming at the mouth. "Lie one more time and I'll kill yo' stupid ass!"

My mama rushed over and grabbed Nihiyah by the shoulders and held her still. "Look at me, baby," she said turning Nihiyah's face towards her. "Do you have a drug problem? Is this the reason you had to move back home, Hiyah?"

"You gon' believe this stank hoe over me? Do I look like a muthafuckin' crackhead, ma? I'm beautiful as hell, ain't no way I'm using any kind of drugs. Weed don't count because it's an herb and it gets me right. I would never use drugs, she is lying!"

"If I'm such a liar, how did I see you over on 63rd last week snorting coke at the party that Dro threw? You had on a pair of black jeans, a pink shirt and a pair of pink and black stilettos. Your hair was bone straight with a part down the middle and you were with Renee'. She was right beside you with a rolled up bill sniffing that white girl. You can keep denying it if you want to, but I have proof."

"You don't have shit!" Nihiyah screamed pushing my mama off her. Mama fell on the floor and I smacked the shit out of my sister. "Let me get outta here before I fuck one of y'all up," she said snatching her purse off the couch.

Nihiyah walked past me toward the door but when she got to Kimmie, she hauled off and punched her in her mouth. My sister could fight, but she was no match for Kimmie. The punch didn't faze her one bit, she came right back and threw a three piece hitting her target. Nihiyah's head went back with every punch.

"That's enough!" Mama had gotten up off the floor and grabbed Kimmie by the arm.

Nihiyah appeared to be stunned, but she lunged for Kimmie and I grabbed her. "Get yo' hands off me, Ni! I got you, bitch!" She said pointing at Kimmie. "Tell yo' man to watch his back, Nija. He is gonna be six feet under with the rest of his people soon," she said walking out the door and slamming it shut.

I snatched the door open and went onto the porch. "What, you throwing threats now, Hiyah? What the fuck did Ricio do to you?" I screamed at her.

"He put his hands on me just like yo' ass did, sister or not, yo' ass on the target list too!" she said jumping in her car and pulling off.

As I walked back into the house, I closed the door and instantly saw the tears running down my mama's cheeks. She was looking at something on Kimmie's phone and she kept saying play it again. I knew then that Kimmie had the proof that Nihiyah was doing drugs.

"Ma, it's going to be alright. Nihiyah is into something this time you won't be able to get her out of. She was talking about Ricio and I are on her target list. I promise you, ma, if your daughter comes at me wrong, I'm fuckin' her up. She is going to get herself hurt if she goes after Ricio."

"I've tried my best to bring you girls up right. I don't know what happened with Nihiyah. Drugs? What could've happened in her life to make her choose to put that shit up her nose?" my mama said crying.

"Shake," Kimmie said.

"What?" I asked confused.

"That's who she has been dealing with for a minute now. Nija, he is part of Floyd's crew."

My mind went back to the day Ricio's truck got shot up. I had told Nihiyah where I was then she started an argument over money. She was the only person to know our location because I gave it to her. Hearing she was fucking with the enemy had me pissed.

"Who the hell is a Shake?" my mama asked whipping her face.

"He is a guy that is well known in the street, ma."

"So, he is a damn drug dealer, huh? This Shake person is the one feeding her that bullshit! I can't blame anyone but my daughter. I'm not about to raise my blood pressure worrying about Nihiyah. If she wants to waste her life dealing with that shit, she can do it outside of my house. I've learned that you can't help someone if they don't want to be helped. I'm going to have a talk with her when she comes back, then I will go from there. Heat up y'all food so we can enjoy this meal," she said walking to the table.

I glanced at Kimmie's phone and she handed it to me. Watching the video hurt me so badly because I never thought my sister would ever do any drug outside of marijuana. The thing that hurt me more was knowing she was the one who set Ricio up to be killed the day we were shot at. It put me in a bad position because I didn't know if I should say something to him about it or not.

"That's fucked up, Kimmie. I'm sorry my sister came at you like she did."

"What the hell you sorry for? When I see her ass again, I'm fuckin' her up. I couldn't beat her ass the way I wanted to because your mama was here. But she is gonna get it. Watch yo'self because drugs will turn anybody against their family. Nihiyah is going to get herself killed out there. Don't take her threats lightly, them niggas is out to get Ricio and Sosa. Keep all information away from your sister," she said walking away from me.

I heard the text chime of my phone and went to get my purse from off the back of the chair. As I opened the message, it was from Sin.

Sin: Meet me at my house in an hour. Something came up, we can work from there.

After responding to the text, I looked through my phone trying to see if Ricio had called, he hadn't. I tried not to think about the woman Nihiyah mentioned he was with earlier, but I couldn't. Things with me and Ricio was going to be different after this funeral, I had to stand my ground with him. It would have to be me, or the other bitches. His choice.

Chapter 10
Beast

I never knew Sosa had another nigga living in his head. He was always the laid back, mediator in many situations. To see him transform into Rodrigo had my ass confused as fuck. What I was worried about was the fact that he wasn't scared of shit. If anyone challenged me, they had to be crazy as hell. He did that shit though. I chose the high road and didn't buck back at his ass. He would've died had he been anyone else.

We drove to the storage facility and it was stocked just like Reese said it would be. The whole crew helped load the truck and we headed back to the warehouse. The cleanup crew was still there waiting for us to return. As I looked around inspecting the work they'd done, I was satisfied with the results. I paid them and sent them on their way before we unloaded the packages.

With the trucked backed inside of the building, we used a couple of pulleys to transfer the dope to the storage room that only Ricio and Sosa would have the keys to. The room was insulated for this reason back in the day. I had some people come in to make sure it was good as new. Installing another safe was a must because I wanted Ricio and Sosa to have control of their own shit at all times.

My phone started ringing and I snatched it from my hip. Sin's picture was on display and I answered it with no hesitation. When she started talking, I walked to the other side of the warehouse to talk to her. The shit she said caught me by surprise but I was happy too. I had to talk some sense into her ass because she was talking stupid as hell. I hung up from her and went back to help unload the truck.

Once we finished transferring shit, I locked the store room turning to both Sosa and Ricio. "These are the only sets of keys to this room. If something comes up missing, y'all would have to look for the answer between the two of you," I said holding the key up for them to see. "This key is to the front door and this one is for the back. The automatic door only opens from the inside by the push of a button. I've had new cameras installed and it's being recorded digitally. I will tell you which app to install on your phones as well as the passwords to get in. An alarm has been installed as well, if it goes off, each of you and myself will get an alert on our phones. Ricio is the only one that will get a call from the police. Now, I have a key to the warehouse and I had six more made because I know how close all of you niggas are. It's up to y'all who gets a key or not," I told them giving them the keyrings.

Ricio didn't hesitate giving out the keys. When he went to hand Psycho his key, Rodrigo grabbed Ricio's arm shaking his head slowly. "That nigga don't get a key until he holla at his punk ass daddy. I know you and Sosa love his ass like a brother, but me, nah not too much. He gots to earn his muthafuckin' stripes by proving he didn't know shit about what his daddy did. I might have to kill this nigga real soon."

"Sosa—"

"That ain't my fuckin' name, nigga! Rodrigo, muthafucka! Sosa ain't in this bitch right now! The quicker you realize we are two different niggas, the better off you will be. Stop playing with me, man," Rodrigo said with his nose flaring.

"Rodrigo, check this. We've been tight since we were kids, now all of a sudden you want to question my character? Where the fuck they do that shit at?" Psycho asked angrily.

"Nigga, Ricio and Sosa been kickin' it with yo' ass since the sandbox, I didn't have shit to do with none of that. When my lil nigga got murked and yo' pussy ass sperm donor's name came into the equation, is when the red flags started waving in my muthafuckin' head! That nigga is the reason Reese ain't here today and you are the one that's gonna take his ass out! If you don't, yo' ass will be in a pine box right beside that nigga because he gon' die regardless," he said walking up on Psycho.

"Rodrigo, hold on, brah. He knows what he has to do. You don't have to come at him like that, he's family," Ricio said pulling him by his shirt.

"You can trust this nigga but I don't! How the fuck did he live under the same roof with Rod's ass and didn't know he wasn't just a muthafuckin' lawyer? He got to prove to me that his ass is just as hurt about my brother as I am. Until then, he don't get a muthafuckin' key! Plain and simple. Don't go behind my back either, Ricio because the nigga will be deader than a doorknob if I see his ass in here by his lonesome. I put that on everything. Are we finished because I got shit to do?" When no one said anything, he took that as a yes. "Aight, I'm out. I'll holla at y'all later," he said walking through the warehouse to the front door.

I watched the man that I helped raise walk out on us without looking back. Sosa was distraught about losing Max but I didn't know it would hit him like this. We had to get the law on our side quick because I had a feeling he was about to be on a whole other level around the streets.

"Ricio, we have to keep an eye on that nigga, he is on a rampage," I said scratching my head. "Psycho, I'm not about to apologize for the shit that just went down. I've never met his ass a day in my life, but I think he is serious about everything he let fall from his mouth. We can't take no chances with him, holla at your daddy and hear him out. You need to find a way to get all the information you can out of his ass."

Psycho looked sad and I felt sorry for him. It was a fucked up situation for anyone to have to address someone they loved about street shit. If anyone else went at that nigga, he would know what was up from the gate, so we had to put the pressure on Psycho to get the job done. The life of a street nigga had its advantages and some disadvantages, this was a loss he had to eat.

"I'm gon' do whatever it takes. I don't how I'm going about it, but it will be done. If we're done here, I'm gon' head out because I got a lot of shit to figure out," he said taking his car keys out of his pocket.

"Yeah, we're about done. Keep ya' eyes open, I'll holla at you later, young blood."

"Aight. Ricio I'll talk to you soon, brah," he said giving him a brotherly hug.

"Bet," Ricio said slapping him on his back.

"Aight, y'all," Psycho said to the rest of the team.

When he left, I looked at the remaining members. "If there is anything any of y'all want to get off ya chest, now is the time to address that shit. I know all of y'all are cool but this is the way that nigga is grieving. He is rolling over anybody that tries to get in his way. Psycho has to face his daddy and we gotta wait for whatever news he comes back with."

"I don't think Sosa should've came at him in that manner, for real. We didn't just lose max, Butta is gone too. We're all hurting in different ways, I get that. He is coming on too strong right now," Fats spoke up.

"What would you do if it was you on the other end of this shit? Sit there and do nothing? Nah, you wouldn't. You would be in the same mindset as Rodrigo, so don't say he's coming strong, His ass is coming even harder now that his brother is gone. This is not the time for any of us to be in our feelings, walking around this muthafucka crying and letting shit blow over. It's game time." I had to see where these niggas heads were. If they weren't on the same page as the rest of us, they could go the fuck on about their business.

"I'm not saying that he is wrong about what he said, but the way he went in on Psych wasn't called for," Fats said hunching his shoulders.

"I don't think he was wrong," AK said loudly. Every nigga involved needs to be dealt with, plain and simple. It's fucked up that Psych's daddy was in on this shit, but that's the life he decided to live and none of them niggas thought it would come to light. Now, it's up to us, and I do mean all of us, to make them niggas see complete darkness. Max was all of our brother, they gon' pay. They gon' pay."

Everything AK said, I agreed with. He was right, we had to be in this together. I knew AK was all in, ready to make Precious clap. He would be the one that was down for whatever.

"What about you, Felon? You got something you want to say while we're getting this shit out?" Ricio asked.

"I'm down for whatever. Y'all know that I've been riding for years and I don't plan on stoppin'. I'm with AK, we ridin' down on these niggas."

"I'm all in until the wheels fall off. I know how Sosa— I mean Rodrigo is feeling right now. I'm feeling the same way. Rodney was there smiling in our faces whenever we went to his crib. For him to continue to act like he gave a fuck about Reese's boys knowing he was the nigga behind the gun, don't sit well with me. That is probably the same shit going through Psych's head too. I think Rodrigo going hard at him is what he needed to get the wheels turning in his head about his ass. Do I feel it was the wrong move to make? Hell nawl! It's part of the game, if he didn't want to deal with the circumstances, he should've left this street shit alone when Rodney told him to. Now he has to put in personal work, it's the life he chose to live. I love Psych with everything in me but, if he don't handle that shit, he gots to go!"

Face chimed in without being asked and I was proud of that shit. From the responses we received, Fats was the one I would have to watch closely. He had a little pussy in him and I smelled it a mile away.

"Get ya head on right, Fats. Ain't shit gon' happen to Psych because he is thorough with his shit. he is his brother's keeper and I'll stand by that shit. We have been his family for many years, especially since his mother died. We all he got. Rodney basically disowned him once he wouldn't leave the streets alone. There's some pent up frustration inside of him for that nigga, it's time for him to let it out." Ricio said.

"I'm cool, fam. I'm with y'all all the way with this shit. I just wish Sosa would bring his ass back because his evil twin is crazy than a muthafucka," Fats said pacing back and forth.

"We're done here so y'all can head on out. Keep them phones on because you could be getting a call at any time. Like I told Psych, keep ya' eyes open. Shit is real out here," I said while looking at the time on my watch.

Everyone said their goodbyes and Ricio and I were the last to leave out of the warehouse. He was locking up when

I remembered the conversation I had with Sin earlier. Waiting for him to finish what he was doing, I leaned up against my car.

"What time do we have to take the truck back to U-Haul?" I asked.

"Oh, we don't. I bought that muthafucka from them. I don't know what we may need it for, but we got that bitch," he laughed as he checked to make sure the door was secured and walked over to where I was.

"Aye, I need you to follow me to the crib. Sin called while we were unloading and she picked Madysen up from the hospital. She's seven months pregnant, nephew."

"Hold up, I just saw Madysen at the party, she didn't look pregnant at all. How the hell is she pregnant and not say shit to nobody? Max didn't even let that cat out the bag."

"I don't know about any of that, what I do know is she can't go back to her apartment. Those niggas know where she lives. We are going to get some of her things from her apartment, but I have to swing by the crib first to get her keys."

"Cool, I'll trail you then we can hop in your whip and take care of that. I'm happy that lil nigga left a part of him behind but it would've been much better if he was still here to enjoy this moment with us. We gon' hold her down like I know he would've done," Ricio looked up at the sky and smiled.

"No doubt, we got her, nephew. She will be straight after we send Max off like the real muthafucka he was. It's about to be hard, but we will get through it. All of us will feel better once we send them niggas to hell," I said opening the door to my ride.

***

I parked my car in the driveway with Ricio right behind me. He got out of his car and stood staring at the other car that was parked next to mine. We walked to the door and I let myself in. the sound of someone sniffling could be heard and I rushed forward to the living room. The coffee table was littered with papers and pens.

Sin and Nija were sitting on the floor while Madysen sat curled in the corner of the couch with a fist full of tissue in her hand. Her eyes were bloodshot red and puffy as tears continued to fall from them. I walked over to her and sat down pulling her into a tight hug.

"Stop all that crying, you gon' be good. You will stay here with us so you won't have to worry about being by yourself. I need your keys, I'm going to your apartment to get some of your stuff. Is there anything specific you need me to bring back?"

"No, what I want can't be brought back," she wailed into my chest. I felt her pain and she was right, there was no way to bring Max back.

"I know it hurts, Madysen, but this is what happens in the game of life. We all have a time when we will leave the world of the living, nobody knows when that time will come. It was Max's time. He was taken from us too soon but there's nothing we can do to change that. From here on out, you have to take care of yourself for the baby's sake. It's not about only you anymore, the baby needs you to be healthy so it can be well. You are not alone. It may feel like you are, but we got you."

"I keep telling her ass but she ain't trying to hear what I have to say. She's talking a lot of crazy shit and it's getting on my damn nerve," Sin said looking over at us on the couch.

"Sin, would you let me do this please. I told you on the phone what I needed you to do. Please don't piss me off, okay."

"Whatever, Erique, she better get with the program. I don't have time for all of the I don't wanna live talk. Life is snuffing muthafuckas out enough, but she wants to be selfish thinking only about her damn self. She got a whole baby inside of her and she don't want to live."

Sin was pissed and I was trying to lighten the mood because the last thing I needed was for her to get mad. She was almost there but I had to put out the fire before it turned into an inferno. "Sin, we have to work together to get her through this. It's not easy and we still have a whole funeral to get through. Give her time, babe."

"Madysen, we will be here for you, boo. Have you eaten?" Nija asked softly.

"No, I'm not hungry," she replied.

"She's been saying the same shit since we left the hospital and that was hours ago. Don't nobody got time to be pacifying no grown ass woman. She better wake the fuck up," Sin said rolling her eyes.

"Sin! What the fuck did I tell you?" I barked.

"And what the fuck did I tell yo' ass?" she snapped back. I wasn't going there with her, I would deal with that shit later.

"You have to eat. The baby needs nutrients and so do you. I'll go see what I can whip up for you," Nija said standing up and walking around Ricio.

She didn't acknowledge the man at all and he was looking crazy in the face. Nija continued to the kitchen and Ricio was right behind her. "Ricio don't follow me around this muthafucka. Go back in the other room," I heard Nija say.

"You ain't talking bout shit, shut up," Ricio said smoothly. I laughed at the two of them because he'd done something to irritate her and she was about to give his ass the blues.

"Are y'all making progress on the arrangements, bae?"

"Yes, we are. I will be going to the funeral home tomorrow—" Sin paused because Madysen started crying again. "Go to the guest room down the hall, that way!" she said pointing in the direction of the room.

Madysen got up and did what she was told and I was about to curse Sin's ass out. She acted like she had no empathy for the girl's damn feelings and it wasn't right. I waited until I heard the door to the guest room close before I said anything to her.

"Didn't I tell yo' ass to put all that cold hearted shit away for a while? Madysen is hurting like a muthafucka and you just keep going at her like she is strong like you! Sin, we have to keep her in a good head space and be there for her. With the shit that keeps coming out of your mouth when you talk to her, she may be taking that as you don't care. You know she is on the brink of doing something stupid and you are pushing her towards it. Stop that shit, man!"

"Beast, I'm not about to hold her hand while she sits around waddling in her sorrows. I'm trying to get her to understand that she has something besides Max to live for but she ain't listening. She may be pregnant but her face ain't, I'm three seconds from slapping her ass. You are the designated pacifier from this point on. The soft shit is not my forte, I'm a tell it like it is kind of girl. I want you to lower yo' tone when you're talking to me too. You know I don't go for that tell Sin what to do type of shit."

"What you gon' do is make me fuck you up. I'm leaving to go to Madysen's crib, I'll be back. I hope you have a better attitude when I return. We'll talk about the arrangements then, maybe then you will be in a better mood. Sin, don't say anything out of the way to that girl, I'm warning you," I said getting up to go get Madysen's keys.

"Don't put a warning label on me. You already know I dance to one drum and that's mine. Go do what you're set out to do, I'll be here," she said without looking up.

As I passed the kitchen, Ricio was talking quietly to Nija and she was ignoring the fuck out of him. I didn't know what happened and didn't really care, he needed to stop playing with her because I had a feeling, she was going to be the one that breaks his ass down.

"Ricio, we bout to be out when I come from the back. Be ready," I said loud enough for him to hear but he kept talking to Nija.

I got the keys from Madysen and made my way back to the front of the house. I heard Nija's voice and I paused. She was giving Ricio a tongue lashing he wasn't ready for. I stood at the entrance of the kitchen and waited.

"I'm not about to play second fiddle another minute for you and your hoes, Ricio. You want to entertain these bitches, do that but leave me out of it. I will be here as long as you need me to be, but after this funeral, I'll be moving on with my life. It's on you now to prove that I'm all the woman you need. The same way you out here living your life, is the way I plan to live mine. My world revolved around you and you took it for granted thinking I wouldn't move around on your ass. You won't have to find out what I'm gonna have going on, I'll let you in on the shit myself. As of today, it's just Mauricio and Nija that's it."

117

"Nija, I don't know what this is about but we need to talk about it. All that shit you saying ain't even relevant right now. I need you here with me to help me through this shit I'm going through."

"I already told you I won't turn my back on you during this time. But afterward, you can seek comfort from whatever bitch you decide to chill with, I'm done." He grabbed her by the shoulders and turned her around to face him. "Don't touch me! Beast is ready to go," she said turning her back to him again.

"I'll see you when I come back to get my car," he said bending down to kiss her temple.

"No, you won't because I won't be here," she said dodging his kiss.

"Where you going, Nija?"

"None of your business! Beast, take his ass out of here before I lay hands on him, please."

"Come on man, so I can get back here. Are you strapped?" I asked him.

"My bitch on me like an American Express card, never leave home without it," he said walking past me. "Nija, I love you girl, "he shouted over his shoulder.

"Kiss my ass, Ricio."

"I will when I get back. Lick you all between your ass cheeks, baby."

Laughing as I followed him out the door, "You a damn fool, nephew. Stop playing with that girl, I think she's serious about what she said to yo' ass."

"Nija ain't going nowhere, Beast. We've been through too much shit for her to leave me alone. It's not like she didn't know how I was beforehand. I'm not worried about her leaving."

118

"Don't come to me with your dick between your legs when she moves the fuck on because you're playing with her muthafuckin' emotions," I said popping the locks on my whip.

I rolled down the street and hopped on the expressway to Madysen's house. When I hit 39th street twenty minutes later, I got out and used the key to get in the entry door. She lived on the second floor and we climbed the stairs slowly. Her apartment was on the right side of the stairs and the door was slightly open. I turned my head with my finger to my lips and took my bitch from my hip. Ricio followed suit.

Easing to the door, I pushed it open slowly and stepped over the part of the floorboard that I knew creaked. Somebody was still in that muthafucka and I could hear them throwing shit around. Screwing the silencer on my gun, I crept further into the apartment.

"That bitch don't got shit in here, man. Let's go. I told you that nigga Max didn't stash his shit here."

I didn't know who the voice belonged to but it didn't matter because they were somewhere they didn't have any business being. One thing I hated was a bitch nigga preying on women. We moved through the apartment and it looked like a hurricane came through and swept everything around.

"Floyd said to come here and see if that nigga left any incriminating evidence in this bitch. I wanted his money and shit for myself. I was going to give you half, but ain't shit here. We came on a blank mission because he didn't even tell me exactly what to look for. Just keep looking, this is the last room we have to search. You checked the kitchen, right?"

"Nope. I thought you did."

"Go check the whole kitchen dumb ass! Damn man, you slow as fuck."

Ole boy came out of the back room and I scooped his ass up by his neck and stuck my steel dick in his mouth. "Don't say shit, nigga," I sneered at him. His eyes grew three times the size and I think he was pissing on himself. I looked around the room and spotted a sheet on the couch. "Get that sheet over there, Nephew," I whispered to Ricio.

After tying his ass up to a chair and sticking a pair of dirty socks in his mouth, both of us made our way to the bedroom. The other nigga was still rummaging through the dresser drawers with his back turned to us. Ricio walked behind him and hit his in the back of his head with his .45. He fell on the floor holding his head groaning loudly.

"Where the fuck is Floyd's bitch ass?" Rico asked bending down yanking him up. When he saw the dudes face, he smiled wickedly. "That nigga keep sending you weak niggas to do a man's job," he laughed. "Joe, when you gon' stop letting that nigga send you on blank missions and shit? Don't answer that, this is your last rodeo nigga. Bring yo' ass on!" he said pushing him out the door.

I flipped the switch and flooded the small living room with light. Madysen wouldn't be able to come back to the apartment after we killed these niggas for sure. They had some explaining to do and I need to know where their leader was.

"I'm gon' ask you again, where the fuck is Floyd?" Ricio barked.

"I don't know, he called and said we needed to come break in Max's girl's house to see what we find. He said something about incriminating evidence but I don't know what he's looking for. I only came because I thought Max stashed his shit here," Joe said.

"Mmmm, mmmmm," the dude that we tied up was mumbling trying to say something. I walked over to him and took the sock out his mouth and pointed my gun at his head.

"What the fuck you trying to say, youngin?"

"That nigga is at the Shamrock motel on 12th and Cicero. I don't have nothing to do with this. Joe asked me to come with him and I did. Floyd is laying low because he is about to come for y'all from the shit Joe told me. His plan is to catch y'all one by one right along with anybody that roll with ya'll. He got his eye on y'all families too."

"Shut the fuck up Bari! Yo' ass singing like a bird and they gon' kill us anyway, stupid muthafucka!"

Chuckling, Ricio hit that nigga in his mouth with the butt of his gun, making him swallow a couple teeth in the process. Joe's head fell down and he was coughing uncontrollably, I guess a tooth went down the wrong pipe.

"Nah nigga, yo' ass talk too much. What else they got planned Bari? You are the only one cooperating, Joe is the only one that won't make it out of here," I told him that shit because I had him right where I wanted his ass.

"He's lying, Bari!" Joe said with blood running down his chin.

"Floyd got some dude that I've never seen before on his side. He made the mistake of not hanging up after he confirmed that everything was straight on the streets. Shake had his phone on speaker and I heard the name Rod or something like that. They were saying how he would be the one to get close to Ricio and Sosa because they wouldn't suspect him of doing anything."

"Bari, shut the fuck up!" Joe yelled. I didn't tolerate bitch ass thug niggas and he was hollering for nothing. Jerking my head to the side, Ricio got the hint and stepped to his left. "These niggas are out for blood and you just ran down damn near the whole operation. I'm fuckin' you up when we get wherever we end up. You need to learn how to close your—"

Pop pop pop. Sending three slugs into Joe's face, he fell on the carpeted floor with a thud. I couldn't stand listening to his whiny ass. I turned back to Bari and he looked like he was about to shit on himself.

"I have one more question for you before I let you leave with yo' life, okay?" He shook his head yes as he shifted his feet in front of him. "How many of Floyd's traps are still up and running?"

"The one on 26th and there is four people running it. The trap on 16th and Central has three niggas running it. The one on Washington and Kostner is still running but there is usually five or six people in there. I don't know nothing about the traps on the Southside. Joe knew all about that but he's dead."

The lil muthafucka had the audacity to let out a long sigh like he had been waiting to get that shit off his chest. All the information he gave us was useful. I was mentally storing all of that shit in my head because a plan was in motion.

"Did they change anything in any of the traps, like the stash spots or the safe codes?" Ricio asked.

"Nah, everything is still the same. Floyd hasn't been to any of the traps since early Friday. We have been contacting him by phone."

The canary continued to sing not knowing he was digging a deeper hole for himself. Bari was talking so fast that he forgot he told us he didn't have nothing to do with any of this. But his ass had all the answers to my questions.

"Aight, lil homie you did good. Keep ya mouth closed and get the fuck out of my city. If I find out yo' ass went back and ran ya mouth, I'm killing yo' whole muthafuckin' family until I find yo' bitch ass. Get the fuck outta hear before I change my mind," Ricio said as he screwed a silencer on his Nina.

I untied him from the chair and stood back. Bari stood up and walked slowly toward the door, looking back to see what we were doing. When he reached for the knob, Ricio delivered two slugs in the back of his head. As he fell to the floor the blood splatter on the door told me at least one bullet exited out the front of his dome. Play time was over for all them niggas.

"Yo', I need a deep cleaning on Pershing. I spilled a whole bottle of wine on the carpet. I'm about to shoot the location, get here asap," Ricio disconnected the call and pushed a few buttons and put his phone in his pocket. "I'll buy Madysen everything she needs, I'm not taking shit out of this bitch. They can clean up this mess and I'll bring the U-Haul back after the service and pack all of it up." The cleanup crew showed up thirty minutes later and we left them to do what we paid them to do.

Chapter 11
Big Jim

I'd been sitting in my cell for the last couple days because Max's death was on my mind heavily. Ricio and his crew wasn't playing out there. Floyd called and said he sent Joe and Bari to that bitch Madysen's crib and they hadn't showed up since Saturday. It was Monday and still no word on them. I already knew both of them were never going to be found again.

Shit had been quiet for the most part but that only meant there was something brewing on the back burner. I told Floyd to get his ass back to Chicago, he claimed he did but nobody had seen him. Everybody I've talked to said the same thing, "I've talked to him, but I haven't seen him," If I was out of this damn prison, I'd kill him myself. Grown ass nigga running scared from some young muthafuckas.

I got up and slipped my shoes on to get out of the cell for a while. Floyd hadn't gotten word on when the funeral was going to be so I was sitting waiting to get a date. As I entered the day room the tv was on channel 9 news. The reporter was outside of Paradise Kitty so I knew the segment was about Max's murder.

"Aye, turn that up!" I yelled across the room. A nigga named G Dog turned the volume up.

"Funeral Services for Maximo Vasquez will be held Friday morning at Taylor Funeral home on Chicago's Southside. The family wants all that knew this young man that lost his life to senseless gun violence to come out and pay your respects. Bernard Gilliam was another victim of the same shooting. His services will be held at an undisclosed location Wednesday morning. There are still no suspects in the case, if there is anyone with information, call the crime stoppers hotline number that's displayed on the bottom of the screen. This is Meredith Holliston, signing off."

"These streets ain't nothing to be played with nowadays."

I turned to see who was talking and it was the guard named Chuck. "Yeah, I raised that lil nigga. Shit fucked up. Can you do me a solid? I need to see the warden so I can get clearance to go to the services."

"Fo sho. As soon as I go back that way, I'll let him know what's up. Do they know who did that shit to homie?" Chuck asked.

"Nah, his hotheaded ass was probably out there flexin' and shit. I always preached to him that he was gon' write a check his ass wouldn't be able to cash. Shid, his punk ass daddy got the business about fo' years ago. I tried to teach his ass how the game was played, but he didn't want to listen. Look at him now, right up there with his muthafuckin' daddy," I said shaking my head.

"Shid, the name doesn't even sound familiar to me. I wouldn't know who they were anyway," Chuck said while looking around the room.

"Reese wasn't shit. He was a selfish muthafucka that let his money get him in trouble. That nigga didn't pay his muthafuckin' workers and one of them niggas popped his ass. I stepped up and took his kids in when that shit happened to him. I came up off that nigga nice too, rest his soul."

"Damn Jim, you sound like you didn't even like the nigga, why would you take custody of his kids?"

"He owed me! My payday was with them kids. When his wife was found dead of an overdose, they didn't have nobody else. I guess the bitch couldn't handle the fact that nigga was maggot food. Don't go outside these walls repeating this shit, I'll be getting out of this muthafucka soon. I'll find out where you live and murk yo' ass. I'm talking because I needed to get that shit out of my system. I had that lil muthafucka killed too, just to put it out there," Fuck it, I had already said too much why not tell him everything.

"Why are you going to the service if you had the kid killed though?" Chuck asked in a low voice.

"I need to know he's dead for myself. That lil nigga know shit he ain't got no business knowing. My name would be drug through the streets bad if the shit got out. I don't need that shit. All he had to do was keep his muthafuckin' mouth closed and he would still be breathing today. Enough about that shit, I'm going back to my cell. Come see me when you talk to the warden, I need to get this escort. Thanks for listening, remember what I said though," I said slapping him on the back as I walked back to my cell.

"Get out and go do something with ya life," I said to my cellie as I laid back on my bunk.

"I'm not ready—"

"I didn't ask yo' ass what you were ready for, nigga. Raise up," I said cutting him off. When he left out closing the door behind him, I laid back and my mind drifted back to the day I killed Maritza.

Floyd met me at the trap where Reese stashed all his dope and money three months after his death. I was his right hand so I had the code to the safe and access to all of the drugs. Getting to all of his shit was my main concern because his ass owed me and I was gon' get paid even though his ass was dead and gone.

I was the only one that knew he didn't take any of his street shit home where his family laid their heads. Reese didn't like the idea of putting his money in any bank. He carried cash at all times because he was afraid the law could track his shit if he used a bank card. We got to the trap and nobody was there because we'd closed down shop after word got out that he was dead.

Unlocking the door, we walked in and I went straight to the basement and pulled the imitation wall out revealing the huge safe that sat behind it. I rubbed my hands together after entering the code on the keypad. I looked over at Floyd with a sly grin on my face, "We're about to be two rich muthafuckas. You ready to take over this shit?"

"Hell yeah, this shit is rightfully ours. Let's get it, nigga," he said excitedly.

I pulled the door to the safe open and rage built up inside me when I saw that muthafucka was bone dry. Wasn't a piece of a dollar in there. "What the fuck!" I yelled out loud.

"What's the problem?" Floyd asked.

Stepping back, I gestured for him to take a look inside the safe. He looked just as confused as I was and that confusion turned into anger. "Who else could've came in and took all the money you said he kept in there?" Floyd shot daggers at me with his eyes.

"Only Reese and myself had access to this muthafucka, I haven't been here. Hold up, let me check the storage room where we kept the bricks," I said damn nearing running to the other side of the basement.

Reese had renovated the basement of this house and made a storage room in the wall. Snatching the dart board off the wall, I punched the code in the keypad that was behind it and swung the door open and went in. The deeper I got into the tunnel, I knew there wasn't a brick in that bitch. Reese had fucked me once again, this time from the grave.

He was probably standing next to me laughing like Patrick Swayze did ole boy in the move Ghost.

"Ain't shit in here either!" I said walking out and punching the wall. "Reese emptied this shit out a long time ago, that's the only way it disappeared. If I could, I'd kill his ass all over again! This is some bullshit! He took it all to that big ass house he lives in. There's no other place it could be. Come on, we going to pay Maritza a visit. The bitch knows something," I said walking up the stairs without even locking anything up.

I was doing ninety on the expressway trying to get to the money. Everything had to be at his crib, where else would he move it to? Finding the shit was all I was worried about because that was my meal ticket. Thinking about all the shit I had in play was pushing me to search high and low for this nigga's stash.

"Aye, look in the hidden compartment and get that un-cut out of there. A needle should be in the black bag underneath it too," I said to Floyd as I kept my eye out for the law.

"What the fuck you need this for?"

"If this bitch don't give me what the fuck I came all the way out here for, she won't live to tell nobody about this visit. She gon' be a dead muthafucka like her husband. Make that shit strong as fuck too, as a matter of fact, make two. I'm ready to give her a double dose of that good shit. Fuck Scotty, she going straight to the Pearly Gates," I said laughing.

Exiting the expressway, I drove the speed limit because the police didn't play out in the burbs. I parked my ride a few houses away from Maritza's house and cut the engine. Floyd opened his door and got out, I did the same. We walked down the street and I took the needles from him and placed them in my pocket after making sure the tips were on them tightly.

Anxiously walking up to the gate of Maritza's house, I punched in the code and let myself inside. As I climbed the stairs to the front door, it swung open forcefully before I could ring the doorbell. She must've seen me approaching on the monitors. Maritza looked good enough to eat standing there with a scarf on her head. She had her hand on her hip along with a scowl on her face.

"I can't believe he gave you of all people the code to our home! Why are you here, Jim? I haven't seen you since before my husband was killed and I didn't want to see you then. This visit can't possibly be of any importance, so make it quick so you can get the fuck off my property," she said angrily in her thick accent.

This bitch didn't know that her slick ass mouth was going to get her in a world of trouble. I was already pissed about my money, then she wanted to stand there getting jazzy at the lips. Floyd snickered, he knew I didn't like any female talking to me like I wasn't shit.

Before she could react, I had my hand around her throat pushing her into the house. Applying pressure, I slammed her into the wall. "Bitch, where is the money?"

Tears streamed from her eyes and she struggled to answer so I threw her to the floor and stood over her. She took deep breaths and quickly tried to crawl away from me. Grabbing her by the ankle, I dragged her back toward me and raised my fist as I bent over her.

"I don't know what you're talking about! Reese never brought his work home, you know this, Jim!" she cried out.

"The drugs and money ain't at the trap, you can't tell me you don't know where it is, Maritza! Where is my shit?"

"His business in the street was never something I knew about. I don't know where any of that shit is! Oh my God, you killed him for this reason! It was you!" she screamed kicking me in my inner thigh.

"Just tell me what the fuck I want to know and you will live, Maritza. I don't want to have to kill yo' ass!"

"Kill me, puta (motherfucker)! I've been ready since your slimy ass took my husband from me! I knew you were behind this shit. He should've left you alone when I told him you weren't shit!"

"Where is the fuckin' money, bitch!" I barked while twisting her foot.

"If I knew I wouldn't tell your pussy ass! Kill me, Jim!"

"Your wish is my command, bitch! Hold this hoe down, Floyd," I said taking the needle from my pocket.

Floyd hovered over Maritza and held her arms. I placed a pair of gloves on my hands and snatched the scarf off her head and tied it around her upper arm. Maritza had good veins that protruded out effortlessly. It wasn't hard to insert the needle.

The uncut heroin that Floyd mixed took effect instantly, her eyes rolled to the top of her head and she stopped fighting to get away. Maritza was high as hell but I needed her to die. She knew too much and her speculations were spot on. I didn't need anyone to find out I was the one that orchestrated Reese's demise.

"You are going to pay for everything you've done Jim. You may kill me, but you won't get away with any of this. When your day comes, I hope you suffer for a very long time, bitch!" she slurred as the drug took effect.

I was tired of hearing her voice. The only thing I wanted to do was watch her take her last breath. I inserted the second syringe in her arm without making sure the air *bubbles were out. Maritza clutched her chest tightly and her breathing became labored. I knew I had caused her to have a heart attack but that was the least of her worries.*

A couple of seconds later her body started shaking and foam filled her mouth. Maritza's lips started turning blue, her hands were balled into fists, and her pupils were still out of sight. Death was next and I smiled until she took her last breath.

"Don't fuck this muthafucka up and don't remove your gloves. Let's find what I came here for," I said to Floyd as I made my way through the house.

I didn't find Reese's stash that day, but I came up with a plan to get some of the shit I was entitled to. That's how I ended up with the boys. The money that I received from his estate was how I ended up being the man in the city.

"Carter! The warden will see you now," Chuck said from the door. "Come on so I can take you down."

"Good looking, nigga. But don't ever walk in my shit without knocking. The rules apply to all you muthafuckas around here. Respect it."

Chuck led the way to the warden's office and I went in and took a seat. Warden Fitzpatrick was looking at me strangely as I sat with my hands folded in my lap. He sifted through my paperwork without saying anything to me.

"Carter, I was informed that you want to request a transfer to a funeral. Who passed away?" he asked.

"I am the guardian of the young man that was killed Friday. The funeral is not what I want to attend, I just want to say my final goodbyes."

"You wouldn't be going to the funeral anyway, Carter. I can get you to the wake," he said looking through another stack of papers. "The cost of the transfer—" he started to say.

"I don't care about the cost. This is something that needs to be done. The only thing I want from you is to approve the transfer, Sir," I said irritably.

"You haven't been in any trouble since you've been here so there's no reason why you shouldn't be able to attend. When is the wake?"

"It's on Tuesday at 11am at Taylor Funeral home in Chicago."

"Okay, your payment has to be in by Wednesday no later than noon. No one is to know that you will be at the funeral home during your visit. Is that understood, Carter? We will contact the funeral home to let them know what time you will arrive, and how much time you have to be there.

"Yeah I hear you," I said standing from the chair. "Thank you."

"Guard!"

Chuck opened the door and escorted me back to my cell. I was happy on the inside knowing that I would get the chance to see my secret get buried without it getting out in the streets.

Meesha

Chapter 12
Floyd

Ricio and Sosa was running through my lil niggas but it was better them than me, they shouldn't be so weak. Big Jim didn't give a fuck about my well being so, I didn't give two fucks about theirs. I felt bad about not going out to assist them in this battle that Big Jim and I started, but I had to come up with a plan and I didn't have it together yet. Time was running out because Ricio wasn't holding back on nothing.

When we were in Memphis, Red started whining about going back to his family in Chicago and I couldn't let him head back alone. Both he and Shake were the strongest on the team since Rico and Sosa left. I still had plenty of go getters riding with me but they were the two I could depend on to have my back.

"What we gon' do about these niggas, mane? They bumpin' niggas off without warning and shit!" Red asked.

"I know yo' ass ain't scared 'round this muthafucka," Shake said laughing.

"Ain't nobody scared of shit! I think it's wrong for us to be sitting back while the lil homies getting' popped off! That's all I'm sayin'."

I sat back listening to this punk muthafucka slick talking. He was going to say something to piss me off and I'd be ready to pounce on his ass. Everybody on my team should be able to hold their own with or without me. What was going on had everything to do with them not paying attention to the seriousness of the situation.

"All of them need to man the fuck up! We've been hustling and busting guns in these streets for years. There's no excuse for them not to blaze back at them niggas. Ricio and

Sosa ain't to be fucked with but they bleed red just like us. I'm waiting on the day that I get to push one of their caps back. Max was lucky because he was shot from a distance. I'm walking right up to whichever one I see first and shooting point blank," Shake barked.

"You talking all that shit but hidin' out in this motel right along with us! This some hoe shit and I ain't going out like this. The team needs us. I'm gon' roll with 'em since you muthafcukas not trying to!" Red said as he stuffed his feet in his shoes. "It don't make sense, Floyd. You are the leader since Big Jim is locked up! Lead this muthafucka before we all get killed waiting around."

"Nigga, are you trying to say I'm not doing my job?" I asked getting in his face.

"I'm not trying to say shit! How much can you be doing sitting in this fuckin' room! Get shit movin', you can't do that holed up here! You may not like what I'm saying but it's nothing but the truth!" he screamed.

Red snatched the door open and there was something lying on the ground. "What the fuck is that?" Shake asked as he stood from the bed pointing. I looked in the direction he was pointing at the same time Red fell to his knees. He picked whatever it was up in his hands and screamed.

"Noooooooo! Nooooooo! Not my baby, mane! I'm so sorry baby, I'm so sorry. I never meant for anything to happen to you," he cried.

"Red, what the fuck is that? I know that's not a head, is it bro?" I asked. Seeing the blood covering his fingers, I didn't want to believe what I was seeing.

"They killed my fuckin' daughter man! She didn't have shit to do with none of this! She was only seven years old man!"

He turned the head around Tiana's eyes were open and there was a piece of paper sticking out of her mouth. I reached down and took it out and unfolded the paper. Reading it to myself, my head fell to my chest as tears rolled down my face. Wiping them away I looked up at Shake.

"What is it, Floyd?" Shake asked.

"Them niggas sent a message and stuck the shit in her mouth," I looked down at the paper again reading what it said out loud. "Ya'll niggas thought we wasn't gon' find y'all after what was done. Well ya thought wrong! Ya took two from our side and now the count is nine for y'all. Whose next, bitches. You can't hide in my city, remember that shit. Watch ya back!"

Red jumped up running to the bed. He snatched a pillow and shook off the pillow case stuffing Tiana's head inside. He pulled his gun and checked the chamber as he put it back in his waistband. With his teeth digging into his bottom lip, the tears continued to roll down his face.

"They won't get away with this shit! I'm going to my crib to check on the rest of my family, then I'm going to search all night to find the niggas responsible for this shit. If y'all rollin' come on. If not fuck ya'll!" Red said running out of the room.

"Red! Red, hold up man! We rolling with you, wait up!" I yelled after him.

Me and Shake ran behind him but he was in his ride and backing out of the parking lot before we could make it to the lot. I felt bad for Red because I knew how much he loved his kids. He was about to fuck something up and I didn't blame him.

"Come on, we got to go find his ass before them niggas catch him out there solo. He needs us to have his back more than ever right now. They fuckin' with babies and shit, that shit ain't even fair," Shake said as he grabbed his keys and left the room.

Closing the door and locking it, I jogged to my whip and pulled out behind Shake. I pulled my phone out and dialed Red's girl, she didn't answer the phone. Dialing Red I got the same results.

"Fuck!"

As I trailed Shake, I noticed he was heading to Red's crib and that's exactly what I had in mind. We pulled up to the complex and police cars were blocking off the intersection along with a coroner's van. There were a lot of people lining the street, but I didn't see Red amongst them. His car was nowhere to be found. Jumping out of my car, I walked up on a chic I've seen hanging around the youngins on the team.

"Yo, baby girl, what the fuck happened?"

"Damn Floyd, somebody is dead in there. I was just chillin' with Kelly last night and she told me she was waiting for Red to get home. She'd brought the kids to my house to play with mine while we smoke a little. She didn't have beef with nobody," she said mugging me angrily. "Word on the street is, you and your crew killed Max. Is this retaliation for that shit Floyd?" she whispered.

"Don't believe everything you hear and don't repeat that shit again. If you don't know what the fuck you're talking about, stop spreading rumors. Has Red been through here yet?"

"Humph, I haven't seen Red at all. You haven't seen him?"

When I was about to answer her question, the door to the house opened and two bodies were being wheeled out. One was the size of an adult and the other was definitely a child. I knew Tiana was dead, I didn't think they had killed Red's whole fuckin' family.

"I'm about to get out of here. Don't tell the muthafuckin' law what the fuck you just said to me, you could be next if you do," I whispered in her ear. The fear on her face told me she wouldn't be uttering a word.

"I'm about to get out of here, find Red. I have to get my ass to this prison to see Big Jim. We need a plan, my nigga."

"Yeah, we do after this shit. I think we need to run up on them niggas, real talk."

"How do you suppose we do that, Shake? Nobody knows where the niggas are since they left the team! That's the upper hand they have on us. Ricio must've had this planned for a while because he knew everything about us and we knew nothing about them outside of what they did with us. This is fucked up!" I said slamming my fist into my hand. "They can't hide forever though. Max's funeral is coming up and I'm gon' find out when and where it is."

"That's when we gon' have to strike. In the meantime, I'm about to ride the streets and see what I can find out. I'll keep you posted and tell Big Jim I said what's up. Watch ya'self out here, big homie, these niggas are reckless.

I shook up with Shake and made my way back to my ride. Thinking about what happened to Red's family, I drove down Madison Street. I continued trying to reach him but he still wasn't answering. Red was not one to not answer his phone and that alone worried me. His mindset had to be on going after Ricio and Sosa. Dialing up Shake, I listened to the phone ring before he answered.

"Yeah."

"I've been blowing up Red's phone and he's not answering. Find him, fam," I pleaded.

"I'm rollin' to the first spot now. I'll keep you posted, he's all good Floyd. This shit is fucked up and we will strike back. Keep yo' phone on, if you don't respond I will leave you a message. Check ya shit once you come out of the prison," he said hanging up.

The phone was still in my hand as it rang again. I glanced at it quickly before answering. "What's up youngin?"

"I need a hit, Floyd. You got me?"

Nihiyah was Shake's dip off and she came to me whenever she wanted to get high. He didn't know she was a junkie in the making but that wasn't my problem. If she was paying, I supplied. It was all about the money for me. I would keep her secret as long as she kept the money coming my way.

"I can't get to you right now, Nihiyah, you gon' have to wait 'til later."

"Why can't you meet me? I'm standing on the corner of Madison and Pulaski, I can't wait," she said loudly.

"Aight, I'm about ten minutes away. I need you to get in and I will let you out on the next corner. Have my money ready, Nihiyah."

"Okay, damn!"

Hanging up on her ass I drove down Madison and turned the radio on to replace the silence that was smothering me inside of my ride. Shit was getting out of hand and I had to admit to myself, Reese's boys scared the fuck out of me. They have proven that they in fact had the blood of their father running through their veins.

Nihiyah was standing at the bus stop like she said she would be and I pulled up to the curb and popped the locks. By looking at her, one would never know that she was a fucking base head. She was a chocolate beauty with long hair that flowed down her back. Her caramel skin was smooth and blemish free. Nihiyah had a body that women paid top dollar to acquire. With the way she bought the snow I provided, her looks would be history before long.

"How much do you want?" I asked as I pulled to the curb on Hamlin Boulevard.

"Floyd, I don't have any money. What would I have to do to get an ounce from you, right now?"

"Bitch I told you I had some shit to do! Why the fuck are you wasting my muthafuckin' time? Get the fuck out, Nihiyah!"

"I need some coke! I'm feeling sick without it, please!" she begged. "I can find out where Ricio is. You've been looking for him and can't find him. I was going to tell Shake but he has been missing in action but I'd give you the information for drugs.

My ears perked up when she mentioned Ricio's name. She had my attention from that point. I hit my turn signal and merged into traffic, making my way to the expressway. This bitch was going with me and she would tell me everything she knew.

"Get to talking before I push yo' ass outta this car, Nihiyah."

"Give me a little bit to take the edge off first."

"Bitch you ain't getting shit until you can prove you know some shit," I said angrily.

"Okay! Ricio fucks with my sister. She hasn't been to her house since the drive by on 79th last week. I was the one that told Shake their location," she bragged.

Nihiyah was a snake ass bitch to use her sister to help her man get at a nigga, but I'm glad she was working with us. "If she hasn't been home, where is she living?" I asked.

"She's been living with Ricio's hoe ass. I don't know why she is with him because I saw him the other day with another bitch. That nigga put his hands on me and this is my get back, I bet he won't touch another female."

"So, that means you know where the nigga lay his head, right?"

"Nah, I don't know where he lives. That's something she would never let out. Me and my sister fell out Saturday so she may not talk to me for a while, but I don't give a fuck. What you will have to do is follow my sister to get to Ricio. She works at the Illinois Department of Human Services on 80th and Cottage Grove. Nija's best friend Kimmie is another way to get to her too. She lives on 92nd and Sawyer. Make sure y'all kill Kimmie's ass for me! I can't stand that hoe. She told my mama I used coke and it wasn't her place to tell that shit."

"Well you do use coke, own up to your drug of choice, baby girl. You gave me a lot to work with so here you go," I said giving her a baggie of coke. "I'll give you the ounce on our way back. Go ahead and do yo' thang, we still got about an hour to go before I get where I'm going."

Nihiyah snorted the coke straight from the bag and threw her head back after every toke. She was too pretty to be doing that shit, but who was I to tell her to stop. I drove while listening to the radio and she was out minutes later.

I took the empty baggie and threw it out the window and continued on my way. when I pulled up to the prison Nihiyah was still sleeping soundly. My first mind was to leave her ass asleep but I didn't want her to panic when she woke up. Nudging her awake, she rubbed her eyes and glanced around confused.

"What are we doing here?" she asked.

"I have business to take care of. Sit tight until I come out. You can't come in with me because you are not on the visitor list and you won't be allowed in. It won't be too long so just chill until I come back. Shit, take yo' ass back to sleep. I know what's in my shit, Nihiyah. If I come back and you've touch anything and I do mean anything, I'm killin' yo' ass and dumpin' yo' body in one of these corn fields. Don't fuck with me," I warned her.

"Aight! I won't. Hurry up though."

Opening the door, I got out and walked to the entrance. As I neared the counter there was a fine ass bitch sitting in a chair smiling down at her phone. She looked up and stood when she saw me approaching.

"May I help you?" she asked.

"Yeah, I'm here to see James Carter," I said with a smile.

She tapped on the computer and scrunched up her eyebrows. "Um, Carter visits are on Wednesday, sir. You would have to come back tomorrow," she said as she looked up at me.

I looked at her name tag and it read 'Smith'. "Miss Smith, this is an emergency and I wanted to inform Mr. Carter of a death in the family. Is there anyway you can make an exception this once?"

"I'm afraid not, sir. Rules are rules, there's nothing I can do to overturn what's in place."

"You mean to tell me that I've drove two hours for nothing! This is bullshit."

"Sir, I don't know what else to tell you. All I know is, I can't let you in to see him."

Pacing back and forth for a couple minutes, the door to the prison opened and in walked Nihiyah. I hurried toward her and glared down at her. "Didn't I tell you to stay yo' ass in the car? Why can't you follow simple instructions?"

"I had to use the bathroom," she said looking around me. Her whole demeanor changed and I had to see what had her attention. I turned around and Officer Smith was mugging Nihiyah too. "Bitch, if you wasn't behind that glass I'd beat the shit out of you!" she screamed trying to move toward the counter.

Grabbing her by the arm, I pushed her out the door. Turning back around I yelled thanks to Officer Smith and guided Nihiyah's crazy ass to the car. She had lost her mind acting the way she had in a prison. I was already pissed because I came all the way out there and didn't get to talk to Big Jim.

"You do know that's a prison, right? Why would you show your ass like that in there, Nihiyah?"

"That's the bitch Ricio was with the other day! She's fuckin' with that nigga and I'm beating her ass because he was defending her stupid ass when he hit me!"

"Get the fuck in the car before you get locked the fuck up," I said as I opened the door and shoved her inside.

The wheels in my head were turning a mile a minute and I couldn't wait to get Nihiyah's ass out of my car. Miss Smith was going to get us even closer to Ricio. With the information that Nihiyah spilled as well as knowing the connection with Miss Smith, Ricio and his brother were living on borrowed time. Big Jim was going to be happy to hear that this shit was almost over.

Chapter 13
Ricio

Nija has been acting very standoffish with me. I didn't take her seriously when we were at Beast's house but I guess she showed me just how serious she was. Today is Wednesday and I hadn't talked to her since Saturday. When I texted, she left my black ass on read and I didn't like that shit at all. Every time I called, I got her voicemail and I refused to leave a message. She wasn't about to replay the shit I would've said to her friends.

I had to get all the information from Sin about Max's funeral arrangements and that pissed me off because Nija usually kept me in the loop about any and everything she had going on. The bad part about it, I don't even know why she's even mad at me. Thinking about the shit between Nija and myself, I missed the turn I was supposed to take to the warehouse.

After bending the block, I parked out front and got out of my whip. Letting myself inside, I could hear voices of several members of our team. The ones that stood out were those of Rodrigo and Psycho. Following the voices, I rounded the corner and saw the two of them in each other faces. Beast looked in my direction and shook his head. I knew he didn't want me to get involved.

"Nigga, you ain't got in touch with yo' bitch ass daddy since the last time I saw yo' ass! That shit sounds real suspect to me. Any other time that old bastard would be front and center when you needed him! Explain it to me like I'm a two-year-old, Psych. Where the fuck is Rod, nigga?"

"Sosa, I mean Rodrigo, I've been calling him and going by the crib, he ain't been there. I don't know where he at! Don't stand here like I'm lying to you. So, you can get the fuck outta my face before we have a muthafuckin' problem!" Psycho said stepping back a little bit.

"Nigga, ain't shit but space and opportunity in this bitch! That pussy you call yo' daddy had part in my family affairs and he will get dealt with. Do I think you are covering for his ass, I sure in the fuck do. At this point, I don't give a damn how long we've been kickin' it. Blood before mud is my motto and you ain't proving that you're innocent in this shit right now."

"Man, fuck you! I don't—" Psycho couldn't finish what he was saying because Rodrigo hit him hard as fuck in his mouth.

"Fuck me? Fuck me! Nigga, I will end yo' muthafuckin' life, Psych!" Rodrigo said charging at him full force.

I grabbed my brother by the back of his shirt so he couldn't get to Psych. He spun around and pushed me in the chest. Standing my ground, I stared him down as he stood huffing and puffing at me. Sosa knew not to go against me, but Rodrigo was another story.

"Are you choosing this nigga over your own muthafuckin' brother? You already know that I don't care whose ass I beat, it could be yours. Anybody can get this work, I don't discriminate. I think you better be your brother's keeper before you force me to send for the reaper," he said stepping in my face.

"Brah, we ain't about to go there. You already know how I get down, I will beat yo' muthafuckin' ass up in here! I'm not one of these niggas in the streets, I'm a third of Maurice Williams! It would hurt for me to kill my own brother, but don't push me. Give this nigga a chance to get at his daddy is all I'm trying to get you to understand. We have a funeral to attend and all you can think about is killin' muthafuckas. Let that anger out on the niggas on the other side, we about to go shed some blood right now. We ain't killin' our own."

Rodrigo turned to Psycho and grinned at him, "You got saved by the bell, punk. Only because I respect my brother and not to mention, I get to kill some more of Big Jim boys," he laughed. "It still stands though, you will die if I find out you are a mole," he smirked before he gave his attention to Beast.

"Now that y'all are finished beating ya chest, I can tell y'all why I brought you here. We will hit as many traps that belong to Big Jim and his crew into the wee hours of the morning. Kill any and everything moving in all of them," Beast said raising his voice with every word.

"Remember, we are not going in for drugs. We will only get the money that rightfully belongs to Reese," I said looking around the room. "Rodrigo, that does not mean, shoot Psych by accident."

"If I shoot his ass, he will know it's coming. I'm not about to sneak shoot nan muthafucka!" he laughed. "For real Psych, you have to understand where I'm coming from with this shit about your daddy. Handle that shit, that's all I gotta say. I'm ready to hit the road, my trigga finger's itching like a muthafucka," Rodrigo said to no one in particular.

"It will get handled, it won't happen because you're threatening me with the shit though. Stand down and let me do what I do best. You ain't never questioned my get down until now. Does it matter to you how I feel, having to kill the man that created me? It really don't, but it's all good. I'm gon' keep telling myself that you are hurting right now. How long it lasts, that I can't make a promise about. You of all people know I don't bow down to no muthafuckin' body," Psycho said staring directly at Rodrigo.

"Aight, enough of that shit, it's over—for now. We will be hitting traps damn near at the same time. The Westside is where we will start. There are three traps on that side of town. Four of us will go on 26th, and the rest will head to 16th. After those two are shut down, we all will take down the trap in K-Town. I want everyone to pay attention to everything around y'all. We all go in, and we all come out. We look out for one another, that includes you too, Rodrigo," Beast said with a raised eyebrow. "So, it will be Ricio, Fats, and Psycho on 16th. The rest of us is killing everything moving on 26th. Let's go."

"Beast, text me when y'all are in position. Then wait for my signal. We have to hit together, getting in and out fast," I said heading to the door.

Riding in the Navigator, Psycho was up front with me. He kept trying to call someone on his phone and every time he became more frustrated. I watched him do it for about five minutes before I said something to him.

"Give me yo' phone, nigga," I barked with my hand out.

"For what? Never mind, here," he said shoving the phone into my hand.

Glancing down at his call log, I saw that he'd called Rodney numerous times. I pressed the call button and listened to the phone ring. Like Psycho I got the voicemail.

"You have reached Attorney Rodney Baker, I'm not available to answer your call, so leave your name, number and a brief message. I'll be sure to get back with you as soon as I can."

"Do you believe me now, Ricio. I have never lied to you or your brother. I'm sorry for the shit my father did to y'all. He will pay for that shit, I promise you that. Reese was more of a father to me than Rodney was. Finding out he was the one that pulled the trigga did something to me. For his ass to put me out of the house because I was hustling, knowing that's the same shit he was doing fucked me up in the head. Who knows, maybe he's still out in the streets living a double life."

"I hate to be the one to tell you this, Psycho. Rodney is still in the game with Floyd and Big Jim. He's in on this shit to bring me and my brother down. I learned that the other day when Beast and myself went to Madysen's crib. A little nigga named Bari told us everything before he got his brains blown out. You don't have to guess, Rod is still in the streets. Handle yo' business and get him before he gets you," I said glancing in his direction.

Shaking his head, Psycho face hardened. "You mean to tell me he is in cahoots with this shit? He knows I am down with y'all so you telling me this only means he is out to get at me too. Yeah, I have to find his ass to find out what is going on. I'll be going to his job after the funeral since I can't catch him at his crib," Psycho said.

"Whatever you have to do is fine with me, it's Rodrigo that ain't takin' no shorts. I know that nigga is harsh as fuck, but you have to understand where his head is right now. Max's death brought the Grim Reaper out and he won't stop until everyone is dead. I hope he save a couple bodies for us, shit," I laughed.

"Well, we are about to make these guns clap loud and light these muthafuckas up in a minute," Psycho said.

When I pulled up on 16th, there were many kids playing. A couple of boys were playing football, a few little girls playing hopscotch and double Dutch on the sidewalks. Looking around I noticed there wasn't any activity going on outside of the trap and it gave me the opportunity to clear the streets.

Parking my ride down the street, we walked back to talk to some of the parents that were sitting on their porches or playing with their kids. I had a lot of respect for the people on 16th because they looked out for us when we trapped on their block. For doing that, I made sure they were taken care of in return.

"Aye, Tony, I need you to get TJ and Daisha in the house. I'm about to light this muthafucka up real quick," I whispered in his ear. I'd always made it my business to inform people about what I did before I did it in the past. It was no different that day.

"You ain't gotta say shit else," he said turning around looking for his kids. "TJ and Daisha! Let's go get some pizza!" he yelled heading for his car.

I went on the porch and approached a chick that I used to fuck with a while back and she showed all thirty-two of her teeth when she saw me. Taking a sip of what was likely Remy from the cup, her girl pulled on the blunt she had and licked her lips seductively. I ignored both of them because neither one of them were my primary focus.

"I need both of y'all to get the kids and go in the house."

"I need yo' ass to come over and drop that dick in my uterus," she said chuckling.

"Today ain't the day for your bullshit! Get the fuck in the house! If I'm telling you to go, then just do the shit!" I barked.

Her eyes got big and she stood up going down the stairs. "Y'all come on, we going in the house. I'll bring y'all back out later."

"Why, ma?" her oldest son asked.

"Don't question me! Get yo' ass in the house!" she looked at me as I walked away to clear the rest of the kids off the block. When everyone was safely in the house, I texted Beast.

Me: We 'bout to go in. I had to clear the block.

Beast: Aight, cool. It's game time, let's do this shit.

I lead the way to the back of the house through the gateway. We moved silently and I pulled my bitch off my hip. The stairs that led to the basement were clear as well as the yard. Bari had already informed me that none of the locks were changed at the trap. Before getting out of my car, I'd removed the key from my keyring.

Creeping down the steps, I eased the key inside of the lock. I didn't know if anyone was in there at the time. Psycho and Fats stood against the wall while I pushed the door open slowly. As I stepped inside the doorway, I saw one of the lil homies named J-Dubb sitting in a chair with his back to the door.

He was playing the Xbox with a pair of Beats headphones on his head. We all hurried inside because at that point, I wasn't worried about him hearing us. Putting my gun to the back of his head, I snatched the headphones off and tossed them to the side.

"All I want you to do is answer my questions. Is that understood?"

"Ricio, I didn't know that Max got shot. I'm sorry man," he said quietly.

"Shut the fuck up, nigga!" I said striking him across the head. "Who else is in here?"

J-Dubb held the back of his head as blood seeped through his fingers. "Tray Ball and Vell is upstairs counting money and bagging. What do you want? I'll tell you whatever you need to know," he said without turning around.

As he tried to sell his soul to the devil, I was screwing my silencer on my gun. There was nothing this nigga could tell me about nothing, it didn't matter. I knew where everything was in the trap, I didn't need help to shut this muthafucka down. Instead of answering him, I popped two slugs in the back of his head and watched his body slump to the side.

I caught his body and lowered him to the floor to prevent alerting the people upstairs. "Get y'all silencers in place. I don't want to draw any attention to this house from the outside."

Going to the bedroom on the other side of the basement, I filled two duffle bags with all the money that was in the closet. After emptying the closet, I walked back into the open space of the room and put the bags by the door. Pointing toward the stairs I put my finger to my lips and Psycho, Fats, and myself walked quietly up the staircase.

At the top, the door was closed and Psycho eased it open and ducked out. Fats and myself followed him and hugged a wall. The radio was on and Tupac's "Gangsta Party" blared through the speakers. Vell's voice could be heard rapping word for word like he was in an audition for the next person to play Pac in a movie.

There were two entries to the kitchen and I took one, sending Psycho and Fats the other way. Waiting for my signal to move, Psych had his gun ready to clap. Fats was bouncing from one foot to the other and I knew he was anxious to get shit crackin'. Taking a deep breath, I held my hand up to give the signal.

"It's about time you decided to come up and help, bitch," Tray Ball yelled over the music. Bringing my hand down, we all rounded the corner at the same time.

"Nah, he won't be helping nobody ever again, *bitch*," I said laughing.

Tray Ball's eyes got big as he looked down the barrel of my gun. Vell reached to his right and Psycho sent a bullet through his hand before he could grasp the gun that sat in plain sight on the table. The squeal he let out sounded like a pig getting slaughtered.

"Shut yo' punk ass up! Were you crying when yo' muthafuckin' ass was shooting outside of Paradise Kitty?" I asked.

"I wasn't there, man. I promise I wasn't there," Vell cried.

I hated a lying ass nigga. Anybody that knew me could say that for a fact. Responding to the bullshit he said wasn't called for. I decided to let Fats put his ass out of his misery. Nodding my head in his direction, he knew exactly what to do. Fats emptied his clip aiming for Vell's upper body. His head landed on the table with a loud thud.

"Ricio, we ain't who you want to get back at! Floyd orchestrated that shit!" Tray Ball said with his hands up.

"He may have organized the shit, but you followed his lead. One band, one sound, right? Everybody is on one accord, right? Now, all you niggas will die simultaneously," I said shooting him in the left shoulder. "I bet you wished you had come to me before you went after me, huh?" I asked as I shot him in the other arm.

"Aaaaaaaaaahhhh!" he screamed as the bullet entered his flesh. Tray Ball was breathing fast as his hands dropped in his lap. He looked me in the eyes and smiled, "Ricio, you already know I'm not a major nigga on this team.

Killing me won't get you any closer to finding out the shit you are trying to find out. I just sell dope and shoot niggas, just like I did with yo' bitch ass brother."

The words were still lingering on his tongue when all three of us pumped bullets into every part of his body from the waist up. When we finished making Swiss cheese out of his ass, we raced to back to the basement door without taking any of the items from the table. Psycho and Fats each left with a bag over their shoulder, I left out, locked the door behind me, and we all walked briskly back to the car.

There was still no one on the street and I was glad about that. I popped the locks and the trunk as we neared my whip and both Psycho and Fats dumped the bags and got in. Driving down the street, I pulled out my phone and texted Beast.

Me: Done. On my way to K-Town.

I continued to drive until I got to Homan. I took that street to Roosevelt and headed westbound to our final destination. It had been a good ten minutes and Beast still hadn't responded to my text. Glancing down at my phone I didn't have any missed calls or texts. I waited a few more minutes and picked my phone up as a text came through.

Beast: Aight, we are in route too. We had a bit of a complication, Rodrigo was hit in the shoulder but he refuses to go to the hospital. I had some supplies in the car and I patched him up until we can get to the hood doctor. The K-Town spot, we going in guns blazin'. No questions asked. Anybody in there is dying. Point blank. We hitting from the front and the back, kickin' the doors in at the same time. Be ready because this is the end until after the funeral.

Me: Is my brother cool? I'm all for that plan by the way.

Beast: His hardheaded ass will live, if that's what you're worried about. It's gon' take a little bit more than a shot to the shoulder to stop this crazy muthafucka. I'll see you in a minute, Ricio.

Relieved to hear that Rodrigo was good after being shot, I droved a little over the speed limit to make it to my destination. The need to see for myself that my brother was good, was my main focus. I made it to the trap in K-Town first and parked in the alley. Sending a text to Beast, I told him where I was.

Me: I'm parked in the back alley. Meet me back there.

Beast: Okay, I'll be there in ten.

"Ricio, we have a lot of niggas that's still breathing after this. We still have the team on the Southside," Fats said.

"I didn't forget. Everybody is getting dealt with, believe that shit. They can run but they can't hide. I want at least one of these niggas to fight back, this shit is too easy. Rodrigo got shot but he's good, according to Beast. At least one of them niggas on 26th put up a fight," I said laughing. "He didn't leave that muthafucka breathing I tell you that."

Well here comes Beast now, it's time to get these niggas ready so they can be fitted for a toe tag," Fats said loading a clip in his .45 magnum.

Meesha

Chapter 14
Beast

Rodrigo was hyped as hell to pull his trigga again. His ass killed six people already and was ready for more. I didn't blame him for the way he felt because I was with him all the way. Sosa would bow down and wait shit out. This nigga Rodrigo needed a straight jacket.

Turning the corner on 26th, I bent the block and came back around. When I parked my shit, bullets started flying from the house we were about to hit. Them muthafuckas were ready for something to go down. Going down without a fight wasn't an option for them. We had enough ammo to give them the fight they were seeking.

I went into straight combat mode and was ready. Rodrigo opened the car door and slid out, hiding behind the car. AK grabbed Precious and got out as bullets ricocheted off my shit. Good thing it was bulletproof so there wouldn't be a scratch on it. Felon had a gun in both hands when he took cover. I crawled over the console and got out on the passenger side.

Analyzing the situation, I thought about how we were going to go at these muthafuckas without dying in the process. "Okay, they were ready for us. Felon and AK, I want y'all to try to make it to the side of the house to the left. Rodigo and I will take the right side. But first, we have to kill some of these niggas because there are more than four of them in there," I said as bullets continued to fly.

As I told them the plan, that shit changed quickly. The door flew open and three muthafuckas ran out gunnin' at us full throttle. Rodrigo sprang into action and delivered a head shot to the first dude that popped off a couple of rounds as he descended the steps. He fell instantly and the niggas behind him had to hop over his body. That gave us an opportunity to retaliate but it was short lived.

Muthafuckas came from the directions I'd directed my team to go whenever we could get there. We couldn't get a shot off, all we could do was crouch behind the car using it as a shield. "Where the fuck did all these niggas come from?" Felon asked looking through the window.

"I don't know! Don't jump out, let them muthafuckas use their ammo. Stupid muthafuckas ain't realizing they ain't bust not one window to this bitch, but they won't be able to shoot forever," I said watching them fire away.

"Fuck that, we didn't come here to be sitting ducks! Let's eliminate some of these pussies and do what the fuck we came to this muthafucka to do!" Rodrigo barked.

"I'm with Rodrigo," AK agreed. "This is what's gon' happen, I'm about to fuck their asses up with Precious, then y'all come and finish them off. That's the only way," he said. My bitch is birthin' a hunnid round clip, it's only about thirteen of them niggas. We got this, Beast. If we wanna live, we got to fight back!"

"Aight, set it up! We got yo' back. Don't put yo'self in a situation where you can't dip back," I said as he got Precious ready to twerk her big ass.

At that moment, the bullets were coming slower than before and I knew that was our chance to get at them niggas. Rodrigo, with his hardheaded ass, jumped up and took out two with fatal straight head shots. I stood from my position and fired a couple shots hitting one muthafucka in the shoulder making him drop his weapon. AK stepped out and let Precious sing like a gansta rap song on repeat. Bodies started falling like flies.

The rest of us took aim at the niggas that were hiding behind the house and trees. There were only three left and they were playing peekaboo. Rodrigo held up his hand to stop AK from shooting. He ran toward the tree with his gun raised and popped the nigga hiding there in the left temple. His ass hit the ground hard busting what was left of his head open.

Out of my peripheral I saw the muthafucka I'd shot in the shoulder take aim at Rodrigo but I didn't react fast enough to stop him from letting a single shot off. Rodrigo stumbled and hid behind the tree and reloaded his gun. I ran up on the nigga on the ground and emptied my clip into his ass. He wouldn't shoot nobody else. The two remaining niggas ran to the back of the trap. We gave chase but their asses were long gone.

"Those were some of them Southside niggas. It's all good, their time is coming. Fuckin' with Floyd and Big Jim, they're already dead," I said walking back to my ride.

Rodrigo didn't follow us back to the street. Instead he went into the house and five minutes later he came back out with a couple garbage bags and jogged to the car. "Pop the trunk, we gotta get the fuck away from here before the law comes," he said going to the back of my whip.

"We don't have nothing to worry about. The law ain't comin', they in y'all pockets now," I said getting in the driver's seat.

Rodrigo got in and his arm was bleeding badly. I got out and went to the trunk and got my first aid kit. With it in my lap I drove away from the scene pulling over once we got on the expressway. I needed to stop the bleeding the best I could until we got to the hood doctor.

Rolling his shirt sleeve up, I noticed the bullet went straight through. A clean shot. I poured some antiseptic on the wound and his crazy ass didn't even flinch. I packed it and wrapped his arm with gauze for the time being.

"We have to get you to the hood doctor now, Rodrigo. I don't know how long this gauze will hold and you need stitches," I said as I taped the gauze in place.

"Do I look like I'm dying, Beast? This shit can wait, we got moves to make and I'm not missing out on it. Drive this muthafucka and get me to some more bodies."

I wanted to punch him in his shit but I had to remember he wasn't himself. Letting that shit slide, I merged back into traffic and pushed my whip to the Westside. My phone chimed and a message from Ricio came through. Responding I explained Rodrigo getting shot and that we were on our way to the next destination.

So far taking down Big Jim's empire had been a piece of cake, but I had a feeling shit was going to get worse before it got better. Ricio texted me again letting me know they were waiting in the back alley. I pulled up behind his car and got out. When Rodrigo got out and Ricio saw the blood on his shirt, he rushed over to him quickly.

"You good, brah? Let me," Ricio said reaching for his arm.

"Nigga, I'm good. You won't be able to see shit unless the gauze is removed. We don't have time for all that shit. We got more important shit to worry about right now," he said snatching away. "Y'all go to the front door and we will hit the back, kick that bitch in after twenty seconds. We hittin' these niggas wit no hesitation. Don't slip because the last trap knew we were comin' and they were ready. Keep y'all eyes wide the fuck open," Rodrigo said snatching out his twin Nina's.

We split up and when we heard the front door cave in, I kicked the back door once and it flew open. It was quiet as fuck inside the trap and when I flipped the switch, the lights didn't come on. I knew at that point this was planned and they also knew we would hit their spot.

After clearing the entire trap, Ricio and Rodrigo went to the stash spot and that bitch was empty. Everything had been cleaned out and there wasn't a worker in sight. I was confused as to how they would know we were coming that particular day.

"These nigga's were tipped off, but how?" I said out loud.

"Shit, I don't know but I'll find out," Ricio said eyeing Psycho.

"I'm tired of you niggas thinking I'm a snitch ass nigga! Stop comin' for me every muthafuckin' time something goes wrong in y'all plans! I'm not my daddy! As fucked up as the position I'm in is, I've been with y'all all damn day! In a minute I'm just gon' let you muthafuckas do what the fuck y'all want to do anyway. Just know, I'm not going out like a pussy! We all gon' die when the shit comes to it. This didn't have shit to do with me!" Psycho said speaking his mind.

"Nah, nigga this didn't have nothing to do with you. I think this one may be mine," Rodrigo said laughing.

"What the fuck did you do, Rodrigo?" Ricio asked angrily.

"I made them niggas, come out of hiding. That's what the fuck I did! Y'all sitting around twiddling y'all thumbs waiting for their asses to come to y'all, ain't nobody got time for that bullshit! I went to that nigga Red's crib. His bitch opened the door and I found out where that nigga was. After killing that bitch and her kids, I delivered his daughter's head to his ass at the motel they were at. Nothing major," he said putting a stick of gum in his mouth.

"We knew that shit already, brah. All you had to do was ask," Ricio said walking up on him. "You need to calm yo' ass clean the fuck down! You got nine bodies on your hands, stop going out by yo' damn self!"

"If I didn't move, we would still be in the same position that we were when this shit first started. I've killed more muthafuckas than everybody as a whole. Get out my face and get ya weight up. Instead of being in my face you should be putting' your foot in that niggas ass," Rodrigo said pointing at Psycho. "I dare you tell me to do what I've been wanting to do. Ain't shit here, lets ride," Rodrigo laughed walking out the back door.

"We definitely need to get him some help," Felon said sadly. "I understand he wants justice for Max, shit we all do. But every time we've met up, his ass done killed ump-teen mufuckas, that shit is some borderline serial killer type shit." I couldn't stop myself from laughing because of the way Felon said the shit. He was legit scared of Rodrigo.

"Let me find out yo' ass scared of that nigga," Ricio said walking out the back door.

Rodrigo was propped on the side of my whip smoking a blunt without a care in the world. His ass was crazy as fuck and I hadn't grasped that shit either. I had to hurry up and get his ass to the place he called home before he made other plans. It was time to get ready for the event none of us were ready for.

"Hurry the fuck up! I need to go home and get some sleep. A nigga tired from sending muthafuckas to hell by my muthafuckin' self!" he said blowing smoke from his nose.

"Yo' ass need to go get stitched up. That's what we are doing before you bleed on my interior," I said standing in front of him. "Get in the car, nephew.

"Beast, you are not the boss of me, nigga—"

"Get in the muthafuckin' car, brah! Why the fuck do you always have to battle the people that's ridin' with yo' ass? Listen to what the fuck we are trying to tell your hot-headed ass!" Ricio screamed at him.

I was glad he said something to him because I was about to yoke his deranged ass up off his feet. There was only so much disrespect I was willing to take from him. Rodrigo looked at Ricio, snubbing out his blunt. His eyes remained on his brother as he walked around the car and opened the door. He got in and sat back without another word.

"Unc, I have to go check on Nija, get him to the doctor for me. I can't wait for Sosa to bring his ass back out. I'm real close to shooting Rodrigo's ass my damn self."

"He'll be alright, I got him. Be careful out here, Ricio. These niggas got one up on us now that Rodrigo done killed those damn kids," I said staring at Rodrigo through the window. "We got two more days, then we can get our lives on track. Oh, get the money out of my trunk. Rodrigo hit they ass on 26th. There were more niggas than expected over there too. We laid them down but two got away."

"I got what was rightfully ours on 16th too. This trap was the biggest one of them all, but they knew to get that shit outta of there. They gon' show up at the funeral, Beast. I can feel it," Ricio said looking around.

"We will be ready for their asses too. I'll see you tomorrow at the funeral home for the wake, right?"

"Nah, I don't think I can see my little brother lying in a casket two days in a row. If anything pops off, hit me up and I will come running. Other than that, I won't be there. I'll see you Friday," he said giving me a hug. "I appreciate you going to war with us, Beast. Thank you."

"You don't need to thank me, that's what family does for one another. I owe it to Reese to bring these mutha-fuckas down," I said opening the door and getting in my whip. Watching Ricio drive off, I headed to the expressway to drop Psycho and Fats at their cars before I took Rodrigo to get checked out.

***

After the doctor stitched Rodrigo up, I took him back to the warehouse to get his car and I trailed him home. With the wake being the next day, I wanted to make sure he got there safely. If his mindset was fucked up before, it was going to be ten times that come tomorrow. None of us had seen Max since the night he was shot in the hospital. The only person that had seen him was Sin.

She had been in a fucked up mood since she dropped his clothes off at the funeral home. I was glad she took care of everything because that was the hardest thing I'd ever had to do when Reese passed away. It was something I couldn't do again.

Pushing the button on the garage opener, I pulled my car inside and sat there until the door closed completely. As I exited and walked to the door that led to the kitchen, I could hear Sin's voice loud and clear. The anger I heard couldn't be ignored and I knew she and Madysen was go-ing at, again.

"You haven't eaten shit all day, Madysen! How the hell is that healthy? I will tie your ass to a chair and force feed yo' stupid ass! You said that you would do what you had to do for the baby, but you lied! You are trying to starve yourself and I don't know how many times I have to tell you it ain't about you! Deep down you want me to kill yo' muthafuckin' ass but that's not gonna happen!" Sin was heard yelling.

I took that moment to enter the house and Sin was standing over Madysen with her fist balled up. Madysen was sitting like she was bored with hearing what Sin had to say. Her right leg was bouncing ferociously and she stared straight ahead.

"Sin, step back!" I said grabbing her by the arm.

"I can't help her if she doesn't want to help herself, Beast. This is a lose lose situation. This is her fight and she is giving up!"

Sin, I didn't ask you to help me with nothing. I've said it over and over that I don't want this baby without Max! You won't listen to what I'm saying. That's your problem not mine!" Madysen said shaking her head.

"You don't have a muthafuckin' choice! You're carrying a human being in your body, a whole damn baby with a heartbeat. Bitch—"

"Sincere, go upstairs for me, baby. I got this," I said stopping her from saying anything else.

I knew Sin was highly upset and the last thing I wanted her to do was hit the girl. Now was the time for me to have a one on one with Madysen. She needed to understand the importance of eating and taking her vitamins. Sin left the kitchen and came back faster than she'd exited.

"Beast, you better talk to her before I beat her ass! This is the second time you have stopped me from telling her the harsh truth that she needs to hear. You won't be around next time. Madysen, make that the last time you pop off at me. You may not have asked for my help, but I'm the only one that's been around to talk yo' ungrateful ass off the edge. Tough love is all I have to offer. Take it, or get the fuck out!" she said leaving again and stomping up the stairs.

Sighing long and hard, I took a seat beside Madysen at the table. She was biting her nails and her leg was still bouncing. I cleared my throat and folded my hands in front of me. Madysen kept glancing over at me nervously but she didn't speak.

"Madysen, I know it's hard right now with the loss of Max. There is nothing we can do to bring him back. If there was, I would bring him back in a heartbeat. That's not how life works. Max wouldn't want you to dwindle away in your sorrows. He would want you to live your life to the fullest. He may not be here physically to guide you through the hurt, but he left something on this earth that will love you just as much as he did. That's the baby that's growing inside of you right now. I need you to take better care of yourself for the baby's sake. Sin and I will be here to help you through. Ricio and Sosa are not going to turn their backs on you either. Max lives in the hearts of all of us, but you will get the full effect of him once that little boy comes into the world. I don't want you to give up on life. Give the baby as well as yourself a chance to make my nephew proud."

Tears streamed down her face and into her mouth. Madysen looked like a broken woman who didn't want to get out of the depression that she was in. Every mention of the baby she was carrying, made her cringe. I looked around the kitchen and noticed a plate with fried tilapia, spaghetti, and garlic bread sitting on the counter. Standing up, I walked over and put it in the microwave.

The timer sounded and I grabbed a fork and placed the plate in front of her. "Would you eat a little bit for me, for the baby, Madysen?" I asked. She looked over at the plate and wiped her face before picking up the fork.

Madysen ate slowly but it didn't matter to me, as long as she was eating. I would do all that I could for her. It would be up to her if she accepted what I offered. She must have been hungry as hell because she finished every morsel and I got up and grabbed a bottled water from the fridge. She drank it and stood up with the plate in hand.

"I'll take care of that for you. Did you take your vitamins today?"

"Yeah, sergeant Sin made sure of that," she chuckled. I'm going to lie down, I'm tired," she said walking out of the kitchen.

I put the dishes in the dishwasher and made my way upstairs. Sin was about to talk hella shit but I was ready to shut her ass up. As soon as I walked in the room, Sin was oiling her legs and looked up at me. Her face twisted up and she paused mid rub on her leg.

"You need to stop babying her ass, Beast! This shit is getting out of hand. Madysen needs to get her mind together. I swear on everything I love, if she does something to hurt that baby, I'm gonna kill that bitch," she said seriously.

"Sin, she needs time. The funeral is in a couple days and I believe after that, the healing will begin for her. You have to be patient, baby."

"My patience is running thin. I don't know how much more I can take. It's barely been a week and shit ain't getting no better. I will hurt her, Beast!"

I walked over to her and rubbed the remaining oil into her leg. Sin tried to remove her leg from my grasp but I was done with the subject of Madysen. All I wanted to do was get deep in something warm and wet. Sin had just what I needed to get the details of the day off my mind. I needed peace and I was going to get it.

"Lay back," I said seductively but she didn't budge. Running my hands up and down her leg, I moved upward closer to her honey and grazed her outer lips. A low moan escaped her throat. Replacing my hand with my tongue, I drew circles on the thick mound above her lips. That was her hot spot.

I used my fingers to move all the fatty meat upward revealing her bud. My mouth watered and I moved closer to watch her juices flow. Flattening my tongue, I stroked her a couple times and her back automatically hit the bed. I lifted her legs with the crook of my arms and buried my face deep into her treasure cave.

"Sssssss, aaaaaaahhhhh, yeah," she said softly.

I swallowed her nectar and continued to devour her clit. It grew larger with every suckle I applied to it. Dipping my tongue in and out of her hole, I felt her wetness cover my tongue and I loved every bit of it. Gripping her nipple between my thumb and forefinger, I squeezed tightly and felt her legs tremble. She was almost ready to explode.

"Oh shit, Beast! Suck harder."

I obliged and a sea of her juices poured out like a tsunami down my throat. She was breathing hard and I wasn't about to give her time to come down from the high I had her on. I raised up off the floor and unbuckled my pants swiftly. Pulling my member out of my boxers, I guided myself into her hot hole. Moving in and out slowly, I fell forward making sure I didn't put all of my weight on her.

Sin ran her nails down my back and opened her legs wider for me to go in deeper. I knew what she wanted but I didn't want to give it all to her at once. When she pushed my ass into her, I knew then she wasn't willing to wait. I got on my knees and pushed her legs over her head. Balling her up like a pretzel I rocked my dick in and out of her twat. Making it hit her spine with every stroke.

"Aaaaaaah! Beat this pussy baby!" she screamed.

With Madysen in the crib, I was glad I'd gotten the walls soundproofed when I had it built. Sin was making all types of noise and not giving a fuck that we had a guest in the house. She was throwing herself back on me, meeting me stroke for stroke. The tip of my mans was hitting her gspot repeatedly and her walls closed in on me. She was trying to drain me of all my unborn kids and I couldn't do shit about it. Dislodging myself from her tunnel, I tapped her on the thigh.

"Roll yo' fine ass over and get in position," I said wiping the sweat from my forehead. She turned over seductively and arched her back just the way I liked it.

Her ass was round and looked good enough to eat, and that's exactly what I did. Running my tongue down the crack of her ass, I fucked her hole before I eased my tool back into her warm kitty. Hitting her hard from the back, I held on to her waist and got deep inside of her. Sticking my thumb into her asshole, she jerked back on my member and bounced wildly while I opened up her ass.

"Yes! Get it ready, daddy! You know I want you to hit that shit!" she said as she massaged my balls between her legs.

"Oh, that's what you want, Sin?" I asked snatching myself out of her pussy. Licking her ass for good measure, I inserted the tip into her dookie shoot and she bucked like a donkey. Sin was a freak and she loved when I fucked her in her ass. Putting her hand between her legs, she rubbed her clit vigorously. Her asshole closed around my dick and

I knew I was done after that. Holding my nut was getting harder as I pounded in and out of her.

"I'm about to cum, Beast! Hit that shit, baby!"

"Oh, yeah! I'm right there with you baby. Let that shit go, Sin!"

I rode her ass like she was a prized stallion. Spanking her on her ass made her squirt from her pussy and made me cum all in her ass.

"Aaaaaaaah! Yesssssss!" she screamed soaking the sheets and falling face first onto the pillow. I was still cumming in her ass so I went down with her and rolled over still connected to her from the back. She cuddled up against my chest and I kissed her on the cheek before I laid my head back and went to sleep.

Chapter 15
Rodrigo

It seemed as if I had just closed my eyes when the ringing of my cellphone woke me. Snatching it from under my pillow, I recognized the number from the funeral home on the display. I cleared my throat before answering because it was dry as fuck.

"Yeah," I said into the phone quickly.

"Sosa—"

"It's Rodrigo, muthafucka! What do you want so early in the morning? The wake ain't until later."

"I—I was calling because you advised me to contact you if anything concerning your brother's service arose. Someone by the name of Warden Fitzpatrick from Danville Correctional Facility called a couple days ago. He informed me that a James Carter would be arriving at nine in the morning to say his goodbyes to your brother. Maximo's wake starts at eleven—"

I cut him off because I'd heard enough. "All of that is irrelevant to me, Stanley. This is what you will do. Remember that package I dropped off to you the day before yesterday?" I asked.

"Yes," he said in a shaky voice.

"I need you to get it ready by nine. I don't know how you will do it, but get it done. My brother's wake will not take place. I will contact my family and explain everything to them. Your father won't be at the funeral home until tomorrow so everything should go according to my plan. I want everything set up as if Max's wake is still scheduled. I will compensate you for your trouble."

"So—Rodrigo, I don't want any trouble. My father would kill me," he said in a worried voice.

"Listen to me, punk! Yo' muthafuckin' daddy won't find out shit. Do what I say and there won't be no problems for you to worry about. I'll be there in an hour, Stanley. Don't fuck this up."

I hung up before his crybaby ass could even try to talk his way out of helping me. I got out of the bed and went into the bathroom to drain the hose. After flushing the toilet, I washed my hands and picked my phone up. The text I was about to send had to be believable in order for me to pull off my plan. Knowing Big Jim was coming to the wake, had my trigger finger doing the salsa on the keyboard of my phone. Reading over the mass text, I knew there would be questions coming from everybody about the cancellation of the wake.

Me: Good morning. Max's wake has been cancelled. I received a call from the funeral home and they said his body isn't ready for viewing. I will be heading there within the hour to find out why.

Before I could lay my phone on the counter, it started dinging nonstop. I'm not the praying type but I said a silent prayer because I had to do whatever I needed to do to stop anyone from going to the funeral home. Taking a deep breath, I picked up the phone and read the texts that came through moments before.

Beast: What the fuck you mean cancelled?

Ricio: How? I'm getting up now!

Sin: I just saw him the other day! That's bullshit! I'll meet you there.

Me: Hold up! I don't need anyone to come aid with shit! I'm gon' handle this! I promise no one will die. I'm quite sure there's a logical explanation for all of this. Would y'all trust me for once?

Felon: That shit don't sound right. I'm coming with you brah.

Me: I can handle this on my own.

Beast: Okay everybody, we will stay put and let Rodrigo take care of this hiccup. Let's back off and wait for his call. Nephew, it's all yours.

Ricio: I think you are making a mistake, Beast. But it's your call.

Rodrigo: Fuck you, Ricio! I said I got it! It don't matter what you think right now. Don't come to the funeral home because I'm more than capable of handling this situation. I'm out, I just wanted to let y'all know what was going on. I'll fill ya'll in when I'm done. If I need any assistance, I'll hit y'all in this thread.

With all the things I'd done, I knew they didn't trust me. Everything I'd done was necessary. Fucked up, but it needed to be done. Regret was something I didn't feel for my actions. I couldn't wait on any of them to make a move, that's why I stepped up on my own.

I ran to the kitchen and wrapped saran wrap around the bandage on my arm and hurried to take a shower. Taking a black Nike jogging suit from the closet, I threw it on the bed along with my black Airmax sneakers. I opened the top drawer of my dresser and pulled out a pair of black boxers and socks.

After throwing my clothes on I grabbed my keys, wallet and phone, racing out of the house. I jumped on the expressway heading north. Traffic was pretty light for a Thursday morning and I wasn't complaining. It didn't take long for me to arrive at the funeral home at all. When I got there it was ten minutes after eight. I sat in my car and called Stanley. He answered the phone after the third ring.

"Taylor Funeral Home this is Stanley speaking, how may I help you?" he said in a voice too cheerful for a person working at a funeral home.

"I'm outside. Where am I going?"

"Rodrigo?"

"Yeah, it's me. Tell me where to come."

"I'm coming to the front now, give me a sec," he said hanging up.

I waited until the door opened before I got out of my car. Stanley moved to the side to allow me to enter. "Good morning, Rodrigo," he said with his hand held out. I looked down at him and gave him a 'what up' nod. "I'm putting the finishing touches on the project you gave me and it's right this way in Chapel four."

We walked down the hall and the air was stale as fuck. As we passed the other chapels, I was hoping I didn't see any other bodies laid out for viewing. My eyes stayed straight ahead until we reached the chapel reserved for Max. I walked slowly up the aisle and sat in the middle section while Stanley went to the casket to adjust something inside.

There was a picture of Max on a display of flowers along with the slide show of pictures that Nija had put together. The flower arrangements were in clusters along the front of the chapel and there were a lot of them. I could tell which ones were from the family because they were in a slew of blues and whites.

Sin wanted the colors to be white and blue because those were Max's favorite colors. We all agreed to wear custom navy blue suits with white handkerchiefs and white fedoras. The women would wear navy blue outfits of their choosing with something white. Max would be the only one in white with a navy blue handkerchief and fedora.

"Rodrigo, everything is ready. Would you like to take a look?" Stanley asked.

I got up and walked slowly to the casket and closed my eyes. Glancing down into the casket, I smiled. They did a great job on the body and I had no complaints at all.

"Great job," I said patting him on the back. "Here, take this," I said handing him an envelope filled with one hundred dollar bills.

Stanley glanced at his watch and stuck the envelope in his inside pocket and closed the casket. "Mr. Carter should be arriving any minute. I was given strict instructions not to have anyone in here while he paid his respects. Knowing you, that was not part of your plan. The curtain in the right corner is thick enough for you to hide behind until the guards leave the chapel. There's only one way in or out so they will give Mr. Carter time alone to grieve. He will be given thirty minutes tops then they will come back in to escort him out."

"That gives me more than enough time to say what I have to say. Thank you for all your help. You won't regret it."

Stanley's phone started ringing and he looked down at it before answering. "This is Stanley," he said into the phone. "Okay, I will be right out, sir," he said hanging up. "They are outside. I want you to get in position and please don't do anything I can't cover up, Rodrigo."

"I won't bring any heat to your father's establishment. Everything will be the same way you left it. The only thing that won't be the same is Mr. Carter, but he will still be breathing when he leaves here. Go let the bitch in," I said taking my place behind the curtain.

Waiting seemed like an eternity until I heard the sounds of chains echoing off the walls in the hall. My palms started sweating and anxiety started to kick in. I made a vow to myself that I would kill this nigga if I ever got the chance to when I laid eyes on him. It's just my luck that he was heavily guarded and I couldn't touch him.

I heard the door open and then there was movement in the room. My guess was the guards were checking the chapel before they left Big Jim unattended. One of the guards came to the curtain where I was standing and looked around it. We made eye contact and he stepped back letting the curtain go.

"Clear," he yelled out.

"Okay, Carter. You have thirty minutes. We will be out in the hall so you can have time alone to say goodbye. Any time before your thirty minutes is up, you can come out on your own."

"If there's anything you need, have one of the guards to come get me and I will answer any questions you may have," I heard Stanley say.

I didn't hear Big Jim say anything in but the door closing softly was something I heard vividly. His feet dragging across the floor accompanied by the chains that were attached to his feet, could be heard moving slowly. I chose that moment to come out of hiding before he made it to the opened casket.

"Long time no see, nigga," I said showing all thirty-two of my teeth.

"Sosa, yeah it's been awhile since we've crossed paths. You have always been a slick muthafucka. How did you go undetected by the guards?" he asked staring at me evilly.

"You wish you were talking to Sosa right now. I'm not that nigga, but that's neither hear nor there, James Carter. My question to you is, why the fuck is you here? You and your punk ass crew are the reason my brother is laid out in that fancy ass bed, nigga! Luck is on your side because your body guards are outside in the hall to save yo' ass," I sneered walking up on him. "If it was up to me, I would blow yo' muthafuckin' head off!" I said pulling my .380 from my hip.

"Put that shit away, youngin. You wouldn't make it out of here if you shot me," he smirked. "You don't have the heart to shoot a muthafucka anyway."

"I guess that's why several of your workers are no longer breathing, huh? Who do you think is responsible for all that gun smoke? You got it, the one and only Rodrigo Vasquez, nigga."

"Time is ticking for me, I don't have time for this shit," he said walking around me.

I took a seat in the chair to my left and watched as he crept closer to the casket. Big Jim glanced up and noticed the slide show that was playing. He watched for a couple minutes before he continued forward. Stanley didn't raise the pillow per my request and when Big Jim looked into the casket, he got the shock of his life.

"What type of shit is this?" he asked stumbling into the seat behind him. "That's not Max! It looks like Red!" he said shaking his head.

"That's what happens when a muthafucka takes something away from me. Your soldiers are dropping with every turn they decide to make. See, Red thought he could come for me alone but he didn't get the memo. What he should've done was checked my credentials. Sosa is who y'all know, Rodrigo's the one that will leave ya wondering. I'm like a chameleon, my shit changes with the environment," I said walking up to the casket.

I glanced down in the casket for the second time that day and I actually chuckled. I did a number on Red's ass.

he was laying inside with one of his eyes sitting on his cheek, his top lip was severed off, and he had a big ass 'R' carved in his forehead. The clothes that he'd worn the day he came for me were bloody from his shirt to his shoes. The fingers that were once attached to his hands were lying on the top of his chest. The best part of it all, was the fact that he would be buried with his baby girl. Her head was resting under the arm that was no longer attached to his body.

"You are one sick muthafucka and you will pay for this shit. What did that baby have to do with any of this? When you ran with me, we didn't kill babies, nigga!"

"Correction, Big Jim. I never ran with your pussy ass, that would be Sosa. I'm cut from a different cloth," I laughed. "I kill whoever the fuck I want. Guess what? I want to kill yo' ass too and I will. Prison won't save you, bitch. Watch ya' back because you never know when death's gon' come knockin' on ya door."

"You won't have to wait long, I'll be out before you know it. We can handle this shit on the streets if my team don't get to you first," he said getting up. He glanced at Red's body one last time before he started walking toward the door.

"Hey Big, Jim. When you talk to Floyd, tell him he's next," I chuckled. "As far as your punk ass team coming for me, ask them how that shit's been working out for 'em as of late. See you around muthafucka," I said walking back to the curtain to get out of sight.

I listened as the chains clacking together became fainter before I came out of hiding. A few moments later, the door opened and Stanley appeared in the doorway. Meeting him halfway, I finally held my hand out for him to shake.

"Thanks for making this happen. Now get that mutha-fucka outta here and burn his ass up," I walked to the door and paused with my hand on the handle. "If I find out you didn't do as I say, you will be the next body your daddy prepares for visitation." I said leaving him standing there as I read a message from Ricio.

Ricio: **Come to my crib pronto, brah.**

I didn't attempt to reply, I just walked briskly through the hall and out the door to my ride. Man, I was on a high that I couldn't explain. It would've been ten times better if I could've stopped Big Jim from breathing. I didn't want to come down from my high so I thought about how I was able to apprehend Red while I drove slowly to Ricio's crib.

The evening I tracked down Red was after I delivered his daughter's head to the hotel. It didn't take long for him to bolt from the hotel room and jump in his car. Following him in a junk car I had bought a couple days earlier, I noticed he was heading to his house.

Red was dipping in and out of traffic but it was rush hour and the cars were creeping slowly on the expressway. At the next exit he got off and decided to take the street. Other drivers had the same idea so he decided to cut through an alley. The sun was going down and there wasn't much light in the garbage filled alley.

I drove on the sidewalk to get past the cars and went to the other end of the alley to prevent him from coming out. Parking the car, I got out and peeked around the side of a building. Red was kneeled by the side of his car examining his back tire. I had punctured it so he would be forced to stop at some point. Walking up on him slowly with a hood over my head, I called out to him.

"Aye man, you good?" I asked disguising my voice.

"My tire fucked up and I don't have a spare. Fuck!" he screamed taking out his phone. He tried repeatedly to get ahold of someone one but obviously they were not

answering. "Would you be able to give me a ride? I'll pay you. I just need to get to my house," I asked frantically.

"Yeah, I can do that. My car is parked on the corner," I said keeping my voice disguised.

"Okay, I have to grab something out of the car."

I headed to the junk car and waited for him. He walked toward the car with his phone to his ear but frustration was etched on his face. Getting out the car, I opened the back door as he got in the front. His head was down and he was giving his phone attention instead of the stranger he'd asked for a ride.

Taking that moment to get the rope I had for this moment, I quickly wrapped it around his neck securing his head to the headrest. He clawed frantically at the rope but it was too tight for him to grasp.

"What do you want?" Red struggled to ask.

I made sure the rope was secured and got out. Hopping back into the driver's seat, I pulled the hood from my head and his eyes damn near popped from the sockets. While checking his person for any type of weapons, I let him know just how stupid he was.

"You niggas in the middle of a war that y'all started and you out here accepting rides from any damn body. With all the dirt y'all been rollin' in, you shouldn't trust nobody out here, not even the people you've been ridin' with for years. It's too late to preach to the choir though, this was yo' last ride, bitch," I said pocketing the .44 he had tucked in his waist.

What looked like a pillowcase was on the floor between his feet. Without looking inside, I knew this nigga had the severed head of his daughter with him. I smiled and glanced over at him, he was still trying to loosen the rope but he was not going to succeed.

"She died because you were too pussy to face the music of your actions. Your baby mama and both of your kids are going to be waiting for you when you cross over to the other side. I'm quite sure you will only see them briefly because you have a one way ticket to hell for what you mutha-fuckas did to my family."

I drove to the back of an abandoned gas station that I found and got out. Removing the board from the door that I had loosened earlier, I propped it against the side of the building. I didn't have to worry about the law because damn near the whole block was a like a ghost town. Going back to the car, I held my machete in my hand as I pulled the passenger door open. Red was fighting to stay conscious and I was going to give him the chance to enjoy a breath of fresh air.

Cutting the rope from his neck, Red grabbed his throat as he coughed uncontrollably. I snatched his ass out of the car by his collar and dragged him to the gas station door. He was trying to fight hard not to go inside of the building.

I had a tight grip on his shirt with the arm I was shot in and that shit was hurting like a muthafucka. Red grabbed hold of the doorframe and the sound of his nails digging in the warped wood could be heard loud and clear. My arm was trying to give out on me and I didn't know how much longer I would be able to hold him.

"You gon' have to kill me because I'm not going in that muthafucka without a fight!" he screamed.

Battling with this nigga was something I wasn't about to do. I raised my machete and swung it. His fingers separated from his hands and I let him go as his body fell to the ground. The way he was screaming and rolling around made my heart swell.

"Shut yo' muthafuckin' ass up, nigga! You didn't cry when yo' ass was using my brother as target practice," I snapped dragging him by his leg to the center of the room. *"Where the fuck is Floyd?"* I asked calmly as I turned the battery operated light on, illuminating the room just enough for me to see.

"I'm not telling you shit! Fuck you, Sosa!"

"See, Sosa is not who are dealing with right now. I'm gon' give you one last chance to tell me what I want to know. Where is he hiding out, Red? Don't make this harder than it has to be, blood," I said sitting in a chair I'd found in the corner.

"If you gon' kill me, then do that shit! I don't have shit to live for. Y'all already killed my family," Red cried looking down at his hands. *"I can't believe you cut my fuckin' fingers off! Look at this, I'm gon' bleed to death,"* he said holding up his left arm.

While he sat holding his arm up for me to see his hand, I smiled. He actually thought I gave a fuck about what I had done, I didn't. Instead, I raised the blade and cut into the top of his shoulder until his arm fell on the floor next to him.

"Aaaaaaaah!" he howled rolling around on the floor for the second time in a matter of minutes. Blood was shooting out of his arm and every time he rolled, his clothes became redder.

"All I want to know is where Floyd is. Fuck it, what's the plan y'all got in motion for my family?"

"Fuck yo' muthafuckin' family!"

"Wrong answer," I said jumping up punching him repeatedly in his left eye. I didn't realize I was hitting him with the tip of the machete until his body went limp.

When I drew my arm back his eyeball was dangling out of his head. I let his body fall back and I grabbed his top lip and cut that muthafucka off. I then took the machete and carved a big 'R' in his forehead. I wanted to chop his ass up in little bitty pieces but I already had to collect his fingers and arm. That would've been too much.

I left Red's corpse lying on the floor and I went back to the car. Getting the tarp out of the trunk along with some rope, and a pair of gloves, I went back inside. I rolled him up in the tarp and threw his body parts in with him and tied the rope tightly around it. Dragging his body out the door, I reached inside the trunk for the canister of gasoline I had stored back there.

After putting it on the ground, I took a deep breath before I attempted to pick him up. My arm was on fire and I knew I was about to bust every stitch that was sewn in it. I didn't give a fuck though. Lifting him in the trunk wasn't a problem, but the pain I was enduring was.

After securing Red's body in the trunk, I went back inside the gas station and doused the gasoline around inside. Making sure I covered every aspect of the building, I stepped outside and got in the car. With the window down, I aimed a flair gun and fired a single shot sending the gas station up in flames. I pushed down on the gas pedal and whipped the corner as the building exploded, shaking the entire block.

I called Stanley from the funeral home and told him to meet me there in twenty minutes. He wanted to ask a million questions and I had to threaten to kill him before he agreed. I told him to hold on to the body until I gave him the word to cremate it. I knew I would need Red's ass to show up for a reason, and I was glad I had him.

Chapter 16
Ricio

I was scrambling around trying to put on clothes because the text Rodrigo sent didn't sit well with me. There was no way Max's wake was cancelled because his body wasn't ready. My brother was on some other shit, I just didn't know what it was. My plan was to go to the funeral home to find out.

As I pulled my pants over my ass, the doorbell sounded. I wasn't expecting anybody to come to my shit and Nija had a fuckin' key. Without hesitations, I grabbed my bitch from the dresser and made my way to the front door.

"Ding dong, ding dong, ding, ding, ding." Whoever was on the other side of that muthafucka was about to get a rude awakening for ringing my shit like they were crazy.

"What the fuck you want?" I asked as I snatched the door open with my tool aimed.

"Quiten esa mierda. ¿Es así como saudan a todos los que vienen a su Puerta?" (Put that shit away. Is that how you greet everyone that comes to your door?) my uncle Alejandro asked.

"Nah, just the stupid muthafuckas that show up uninvited. How the fuck did you find me here?" I asked without lowering my weapon.

"Ricio, baja el arma y déjame." (Ricio, put the gun down and let me in.)

Lowering the gun to my side, I opened the door wider and allowed him to enter. That's when I noticed he wasn't alone. My uncles Julio, Sebastián, and Hugo were with him and they all looked as if they came to the states to be on bullshit.

"You didn't answer my question, Alejandro. How the fuck did you find out where I live?" I asked closing the door.

"Tengo mis formas de—"

"English muthafucka! You in my country now, I don't feel like speaking Spanish today," I cut his ass off quickly.

"Spanish is part of your heritage, Ricio. You should embrace it. As I was saying before I was rudely interrupted, I have my ways of finding out anything I need to know. It really doesn't matter how I found out, just know if I could find you, anyone can. See the idiots that you at war with, aren't too bright. It wasn't hard to find you though. What I would like to know is why didn't you contact me about Maximo's services? His death was on every news outlet, even in the Domican Repulic. That's how I found out when the funeral was."

"We have been busy with a lot of shit, that's why I didn't call you. Besides, the last conversation me and you had didn't go too well. You acted like you weren't interested in shit but puttin' my daddy down. I meant what I said to you that night." I stood with my legs spread apart with my arms folded over my chest, waiting for his ass to get slick at the mouth. Snatching my phone off my hip, I sent a text to Beast and Rodrigo to get to my crib asap.

"Mauricio, I told you over the phone that I think the things you and your brother are into is because of your father. I still stand by that. Reese was no good for my sister and I told her many times to get away from him. Had she listened, she would be here today to keep you boys out of trouble," Alejandro didn't know he was opening a can of worms that he knew nothing about.

"Being the nigga on the outside looking in, you didn't know shit about what went on with my fuckin' parents. The only thing you were worried about was the fact my daddy was a kingpin," I sneered back.

"Yes, a fuckin' drug dealer! My sister was better than that piece of shit."

My hand was around his neck before he could complete the statement he let fall from his lips. "If you ever disrespect my muthafuckin' father again, I'll kill yo' ass! Without Reese, there wouldn't have been a Sosa, Max, or myself! Instead of guessing, how about you find out how life was for us when both of them were living! We were her family! You and the rest of your family turned your backs on her when she chose Reese over y'all!"

"Mauricio, let him go," Hugo said grabbing my arm.

"Get yo' muthafuckin' hands off me before I forget we are blood related! You should've given this nigga a pep talk before he showed up at my crib. Nothing or no one will stop me from speaking my mind to any one of y'all," I stated without looking at Hugo.

"Reese was not fit to court your mother. My parents had other plans for Maritza but she was blinded by the things your father could do for her with his drug money. He ruined her!" Alejandro yelled in my face despite the fact I could choke his ass to death.

"He didn't ruin shit muthafucka! He allowed her to be the queen she was destined to be. Reese was there when nobody else was! My mother wasn't ruined at all. You don't know shit about what went on in our household," I sneered pushing his head into the wall. "You muthafuckas were jealous because my mother was happy. She was no longer living y'all the shadows, she was no longer there to clean up after the whole family. Shit I think it was because she wanted to be with the big dick nigga instead of the punk your father wanted her to marry," I said tightening the hold I had on Alejandro's neck.

"That was her job in our parent's home. The females were taught early on how to care for their future husband. Maritza was not being mistreated at all. She left her country to come here with a man she barely knew. Had three black ass kids by a good for nothing ass nigger. It ended up being her downfall because she is now dead!"

Alejandro fucked up when he said that nigger word. I would've been cool with him saying nigga but he dragged out the 'er' part of that word. Drawing back my left fist, I punched his ass in the very mouth he cussed me out with.

"Ricio, let him go!"

I didn't hear Beast when he entered my crib, hitting Alejandro in his shit was my main concern. When I heard Beast's voice, I backed up because I respected him like he was my father. Our eyes connected and I let Alejandro's neck go. Rodrigo was standing next to Beast with the look of death in his eyes. His wrist was clasped in Beast's hand tightly.

"Alejandro, long time no see. What's going on in here, man?" Beast asked walking between us.

"Mauricio is very disrespectful. I see that's something Reese didn't teach his ass, to respect his elders."

I charged at him but was pulled back by Rodrigo and my uncle Sebastián. "In order to get respect, bitch, you gotta give it. I'm a grown ass man, not the lil boy you're used to pushing around. I want you to say one more thing out ya mouth about my father and I'm gon' stomp yo' muthafuckin' ears in, nigga," I growled.

"What you not gon' do is stand here and talk shit about Reese. See my name ain't Ricio, you won't get away with talking crazy to me. Uncle or not, I will blow yo' head clean off your body. Whatever beef you had with my daddy, leave that shit back in time because it had nothing to do with us," Rodrigo said coldly.

Beast held his hand in the air to put a halt to Rodrigo going any further. "Look, I know how you and your family felt about Reese. To put it out there, Reese didn't choose Maritza, she chose him. Reese did what was right when she called him saying she was pregnant. He did what any real nigga would do, he went back to the Dominican Republic and brought her back here and married her. If it was wrong of him to make an honest woman out of her, so be it. One thing I can say truthfully is Reese loved that woman with everything in him. He never laid a hand on her. As a matter of fact, he never even raised his voice to her. Reese was that stand-up nigga that took care of home regardless of what he did in the streets. He made sure his family was well taken care of. The only thing y'all knew was, he sold drugs. So what! It's no different than the Vasquez family selling guns. Oops, didn't think I knew about that, huh?"

"Erique, stay out of this! I am talking to my nephews, not you!" Alejandro shot back.

"See, that's where ya wrong, nigga. I'm trying to be the calm before the storm but if you want to turn this shit into a blood bath, we can do that too," Beast said walking in Alejandro's face. "These boys have been my nephews all their lives. You muthafuckas are only here to drag their father and make comparisons. I'm the reason you're still standing here talking shit, all I gotta say is go. The same way you bit yo' tongue with Reese, I'd advise you to do the same with his sons. Instead of bringing up their parent's past, how about getting to know them as men. They just lost their brother, show some empathy. Maritza was the queen of the castle and her husband allowed her to call the shots because it was her job. That's all she had to do, he took care of everything else. The way he made his money, shouldn't matter. Choose yo' battles because I'm down for whatever," Beast said

"No, this is not why we came here. Max is the reason," Hugo said glaring at his brother.

Alejandro was quiet for a moment. He looked down at the floor as he rubbed the back of his neck. Sebastián glanced at him and took a deep breath. Hugo shook his head and turned toward the window. Julio was sitting back on the couch smoking a cigar, chillin'.

"I've been telling you for years that Maritza was good. I talked to her and Reese twice a week until I was comfortable with her being in the states. Alejandro, you refused to accept what it was and continued to find little shit to nick pick about. You only held a grudge because papí instructed you to do so. You and I both know the asshole papí wanted her to marry wasn't good for her. Hell, he's still beating the fuck out of his wife today! Let this shit go. Like Erique said, get to know these boys, they're our familia too." Sebastián paused and looked over at Rodrigo then to me, "I'm sorry I haven't been around. It's a shame that it took something like this to happen for me to come see you guys."

Chuckling I stepped to him and said, "you don't have to apologize, uncle Bash. It's *that* nigga that should be saying he's sorry.

"Listen, I can't take back my actions and words. You boys are my blood and I know my sister is tossing in her grave at how I spoke to you, Mauricio. She was distant because of the way we felt about Reese but she never left his side. All I can do from this day on is protect you with my life and make Max's killers wish they were never born."

Alejandro sounded sincere with his little speech but I wasn't letting his ass get off that easily. "I appreciate you coming, but we don't need yo' fuckin' help. We got this. Half of those niggas are already getting their ass whooped by my father as we speak. Pay your respects and go back to wherever the fuck you were all these years," I said walking to the kitchen.

I grabbed a glass and poured a double shot of Remy in it. Twirling the brown liquid around before throwing it down my throat, I heard a voice in my head loud as day. "This is not the time for you to be pinheaded, son. Let the muthafucka help you. Use them as your secret weapons. Floyd has never seen Maritza's people, they will go undetected in these streets. You will need them at the funeral, listen to what I'm saying."

Reese was always in my ear and I was glad he looked after me through all of this. Without him giving me insight, we would be fucked. Taking another shot, I walked back into the living room and everyone was sitting back talking.

"So, you aren't Sosa right now?" Julio asked Rodrigo with his elbows resting on his knees.

"Nah, how many times do I have to say my name is Rodrigo?"

"That's funny because our grandfather's name was Rodrigo. He was nothing to play with according to my father. He killed men with his bare hands and didn't care what time of day it was. A pretty vicious man," Julio said laughing. "If you're anything like him, I think I should be scared of you," he laughed.

"You should be," Rodrigo said nonchalantly as he pulled on his blunt. "Y'all lucky I didn't drop ya boy over there for talking greasy, but I wanted to hear him out since my mama loved y'all so much. The blood we share is the only thing that saved ya in here. Don't let the shit happen again," he said staring at Alejandro.

Sebastián took that moment to speak cutting off the tension before it could before it could expand further. "We have five of your cousins coming up later tonight. They are around you and Mauricio's age. There's Nicolás, Mateo, Alexander, Angel, and Javier. We brought the Vasquez clan up to help put these punks to rest."

"I'm all for y'all helping out. A little birdie told me that we could use y'all at the funeral since nobody around here knows anything about any of you. Having several pairs of eyes paying attention to what's going on inside the funeral home as well as outside, would allow us to say our good-byes without having to watch our backs," I said taking a seat on the arm of the chair by the window. "Speaking of the funeral home, Rodrigo. What was the reason Max's wake was cancelled?"

A look of amusement was etched on Rodrigo's face. I knew then he was on some other shit. "I was the one that cancelled the wake but let me explain why," he said hurriedly.

"You better have a damn good reason, brah. That's something we can't get back!" I yelled at him.

"Pipe that shit down, Ricio. Hear me out, damn! Okay, I went by Red's crib the other day and his bitch opened the door. I tortured her ass until she told me where he was hiding out. This is where y'all gon' get mad. I killed her and the kids," Rodrigo paused because he knew that was some shit I wasn't down for.

"Damn, nephew," Beast said shaking his head.

"I took the head of his daughter and dropped it at the door of the hotel. When that nigga came out, he couldn't help but see it. Just like I knew he would, he jumped in his car and sped off. I had already punctured his tire so he would have to stop. To make a long story short, I slumped that nigga and took his body to the funeral home. I paid the funeral director's son to cremate him, but I got a call this morning stating Big Jim was coming to the wake to pay his respects. The body hadn't been burned yet so I had Stanley to prepare Red's body up in Max's viewing room instead. Scared the shit out of Big Jim's ass. There's definitely going to be some shit at the funeral tomorrow, we have to keep our eyes open."

"Yeah, you sure are a replica of your great grandfather Rodrigo. He has to be living his best life through you because you are one—"

I cut Julio off before he could say the word crazy. The last thing I need was my brother killing his ass. We needed all the extra bodies we could with the shit he pulled with Big Jim. "Nah, Julio. Let that sentence fade away. Say it in your head but don't say it out loud for your own sake. Rodrigo, that's nine bodies you got under your belt. Would you please stop going out alone? At least take somebody with you."

"I work better alone. Besides, you muthafuckas think too much. I work off impulse. The niggas on their team is weak ass fuck. They shot me in the arm and the shit don't even hurt no mo'," he said laughing.

"We will get out of your hair and we'll see y'all at the funeral home in the morning. Be careful out here, we are staying at the W hotel, so you will know. Send me pics of the clowns we are keeping an eye out for tomorrow via text. I want to be ready for whatever. We won't be leaving until you guys are able to live peacefully in the streets of Chicago," Sebastián said standing up.

Standing to my feet as well, I walked over and accepted the hand he held out. When Alejandro held his hand out, I looked at it them grasped it. he pulled me in for a brotherly hug and whispered in my ear, "I truly apologize for my actions. Now that I know my brother in law was everything my sister wanted, I feel bad for not really getting to know him. I'm willing to get to know my sister's sons, if you allow me to," he said stepping back.

"I'm down for whatever. Let's get through this bullshit and we will go from there. A trip to the Dominican Republic may be what I need after all I've been through," I said slapping him on the shoulder.

Alejandro stepped to Rodrigo and shook his hand. Opening his mouth to say something to him, Rodrigo closed his eyes and shook his head. "I don't want to hear that mushy shit. I forgive yo' ass. Remember what I said, though." We all laughed at his deranged ass.

"Erique it was good seeing you," Alejandro said walking to the door.

"Hold up, I'll walk out with y'all. I'm about to shake fellas, if y'all need me, hit me up," Beast said giving both of us hugs.

"I'm not staying here with this muthafucka, I'm going home to go to sleep, I wore myself out today."

Brah, if I come to your crib and you're not there, I'm personally beating your ass. You have been lying too much this past week. I can't believe shit you say no more," I said frowning at Rodrigo.

"Oh well, the bitches in the street made me into the ain't shit nigga I turned out to be. Goodnight, brah. Love ya."

Rodrigo led the pack out of the door and I was left alone to think about the day I'd been dreading all week. Seeing

Max laying in a casket was something I would never be able to prepare for. Nija was what I needed but she was still ignoring my calls. Walking to my bedroom, I picked up the phone and went to the *Uber Eats* app to get me something to eat.

Meesha

Chapter 17
Sin

The day was finally here and I was not ready at all. I'd tossed and turned all night barely getting any sleep at all thinking about this funeral. It was still kind of a shock to me that Max was really gone. Madysen and I sat up and had a serious talk and she promised to do right by herself while she was pregnant. That was the only thing that put a smile on my face the entire week.

Laying out the outfit I chose to wear, I looked at it with admiration. The navy blue pantsuit I chose was tuxedo like with wide legs. I had a white silk cami to wear under it, along with some navy and white Manolo pumps. The suit jacket was purposely a size bigger than usual because I'd be damned if I didn't take my bitches with me. I took it to the cleaners so Sue Wang could alter it fit perfectly and look good at the same time.

Beast had a navy blue suit with black dress shoes and a white button down. With his broad shoulders, I had to have his shit tailor made. But that's usually what we had to do with his suits. Beast was already up and showered. He couldn't sleep last night after he got in and spent most of the night in his office.

I got up and walked downstairs to make sure Madysen was up. As I walked up to the door, I could hear her talking. I knew she didn't have anyone in there, but it seemed like she was crying as well. I put my ear to the door so I could hear.

"Why did you leave me, Max? I don't know if I can do this. Seeing you for the last time will only confirm that I've lost you forever. The baby is coming and you won't be here to cut the umbilical cord, you won't see hear him say his first words, take his first steps, see him grow into a man," she wailed lowly. "I miss you so much. It's so hard living without you. I made a promise to Sin not neglect myself during this pregnancy. Max, I only said okay to get her off my back. This is not the way I wanted to bring a baby into this world. We were supposed to raise our kids together."

Madysen was crying hard and I felt a tear roll down my cheek while I listened to her. Tapping lightly on the door, I waited for her to invite me in before I entered. When she gave the okay, I pushed the door and she was lying in the bed with her back to the door. sitting on the side of the bed, I gathered her in my arms and we cried together. Once I got myself together, I moved the hair out of her face and looked down on her.

"We are going to get through this, Madysen. It's okay to cry whenever you feel the urge, but you have to get up because this is one party we can't be late for. It will start with or without us," I said getting up to go to the closet.

Reaching inside I grabbed the navy blue maternity dress out and laid it on the foot of the bed. In a week's time, Madysen had blew up like a balloon. She was huge, but no one would be able to tell she was with child. I'd gotten her a pair of flat dress shoes so she would be comfortable for a few hours.

"Sin, would it be okay if I didn't go? I don't want to see him like that."

"You don't have to go if you don't want to. I just don't want you to regret not going to say goodbye at some point down the line. The funeral is part of the healing process when a loved one passes on. You need that closure, Madysen. We will be leaving in an hour, if you are going, meet us at the door," I said sadly.

I went back to my bedroom and Beast was sitting on the bed with his socks and dress pants on. He was looking down at the floor with his hands folded. This was going to be the day I had to put my big girl panties on and be strong for everybody. So far, there were two people breaking right before my eyes and there were two more that I hadn't even seen.

"Are you okay, baby?" I asked as I sat down. He didn't respond so I waited. Beast was praying and there weren't too many times I got to see him do it.

He didn't seem like he would be finished any time soon so I went into the bathroom to get myself ready. Turning on the shower, I put the cap on my head to protect the wrap I had done the night before. The water splashed down my back and massaged my shoulders. After cleaning my body twice, I turned the water off and stepped out. I wrapped a towel around my body and flipped the switch for the ex-haust fan. The steam in the bathroom was so thick I had to open the door.

I decided I would go natural because makeup and tears didn't mix. Being outside looking like a raccoon was not for me. While moisturizing my face, I saw my man stand-ing behind me looking sharper than a knife in his suit. My lady parts started tingling but I had to check her ass because there wasn't time for all that.

"Hey handsome, you all good? You lookin' good," I said turning around to see him in the flesh.

"Yes, I was having a moment. I'm ready to face this day head on and thank you. You looking mighty good your-self in that towel. Would it be wrong if I taste you before we leave?"

I started blushing like a little school girl, "yes because we will be late as hell because that particular meal can't be rushed. You have to take your time with these cookies. What you can do is check on Madysen for me. She's also was having a moment and hadn't decided if she was going to the funeral or not. Take care of that while I get dressed, would you?"

"Anything for you, beautiful. I'm going right now because if I stay in this doorway any longer, you'll be bending over that sink with your pussy in my mouth," he said wickedly.

"Get your mannish ass out of here Erique," I said laughing.

It didn't take me long to get dressed. Stepping into my shoes, I put my holster on and put my twins in place with extra clips. As I pulled on my jacket, Beast walked in the room with a smirk on his face. I gathered my clutched and put my small .22 caliber in with my phone and keys.

"What are you gawkin' at me for?"

"That's all you packin' today?" he asked chuckling.

"Yes, it is. Why?"

"You a damn lie, Sin. Let me pat you down."

"You ain't patting down shit, take my word on it will you. We need to get out of here, the funeral starts in a half hour. I wanted to be there early to scope out the place."

"I got that covered, all you have to worry about is getting through the service. Make sure you have lots of tissue for your snotty ass nose," he said laughing.

"Fuck you, jerk. Is Madysen—" I stopped talking when I saw her waiting by the door with a pair of shades on. "I'm glad you changed your mind. You will be glad you did when it's over and done," I said handing Beast his fedora and motioning to Madysen to open the door.

The ride to the funeral home was deathly quiet. I felt my phone vibrate after we had been on the road about fifteen minutes. Reaching in my clutch, I took my phone out and it was Nija texting me.

Nija: Where are y'all? This place is packed and I don't feel safe being here with only Kimmie.

Me: Beast, Madysen and myself are on our way. There are people watching everything going on, you're safe. I haven't heard from Ricio, call to see where he is. I'll call Rodrigo.

Nija: I haven't talked to Ricio since Saturday. After today, he can kiss my ass.

I wasn't getting in all that shit with them. She would have to wait until I pulled up. What I didn't have time for was beef. Getting through this funeral was my number one priority. Beast's jaw was flexing the closer we got to the funeral home. He was nervous as hell and it was written on his face. I let the visor down pretending to check my face but I was actually studying Madysen. She sat back biting her nails down to nubs.

We pulled into the parking lot and went straight to the section reserved for us, as well as Ricio and Rodrigo. Beast cut the ignition and took the deepest breath I've ever heard in my life. I reached over and grasped his hand and gave it a gentle squeeze. He raised the back of my hand to his lips and kissed it softly before opening the door to get out.

There was a light rain fall coming down and I was glad there was a big ass umbrella in the car. Beast reached in the back and grabbed it then walked around the car to allow us to get under the umbrella without getting wet. Madysen was walking slowly and I had to hold on to her arm to make sure she didn't run off. When we rounded the corner to the front of the funeral home, I noticed a lot of unfamiliar faces scattered out front.

"Babe, who are those people?" I whispered so only he could hear.

"The Vasquez clan" was all he said, but that's all I needed to know. I was glad Maritza's family decided to come.

I felt Madysen pulling back with every step we took toward the door. She was breathing funny and rubbing her stomach. "Are you okay? Are you having stomach pains?" I asked nervously.

"No, I'm just nervous. I'm sorry," she said wiping the tears that ran down her face.

"Do you want to go to the bathroom before we go inside? I'm here for whatever you need to do."

"No, no. Let's go sit down, I'll be fine," she said as Beast held the door opened for us.

Nija was standing talking to her friend Kimmie when she noticed me walking up. She took one look at Madysen and wrapped her in a hug. Kimmie said her hellos to Beast and I and we greeted her in return. Rodrigo walked through the door with his suit on and his white shirt had the top two buttons opened. His demeanor was not hard like Rodrigo's, that meant he was Sosa at the moment.

"What's up, nephew?" Beast said giving him a brotherly hug when he made it to us.

"Nothing much. You good, Mads?" he asked Madysen as Nija released her. He held out his arms for her to enter them. "Everything will be okay. I'm sorry I haven't been around, this has been hard for all of us. I got you. Don't worry about nothing," he said rubbing her stomach.

"We will wait on Ricio to come inside before we go in," I said loud enough for everyone to hear.

"He's parking his ride. I saw him pull in the lot as I walking up. I saw my uncles outside, when did they get in town?" That proved what I already knew. Sosa didn't know any of the shit Rodrigo put his ass through.

"They arrived last night," Beast explained. "You don't recall anything from the past week?"

"Nah, I was wondering how the fuck I got a bullet hole in my arm."

I laughed because the shit amazed the hell out of me that he truly didn't remember. "Rodrigo came out to play for a while," I said studying his reaction.

I need to seek some type of help, that muthafucka is crazy. He gon' have my ass locked up some damn where."

"Don't let him hear you say that shit," Ricio said laughing as he walked up behind us. "That dude's been wildin' out in the streets of Chicago. We'll fill you in later, we have an important task to complete first," Ricio said.

We started walking toward the chapel where Max's funeral was taking place when Psycho and the others came in and fell in line. Alejandro, Julio, Sebastián and Hugo would be inside while the young Vasquez boys watched outside. Ricio and Sosa were standing on each side of Madysen to make sure she made it to the seats.

There was a long line that had formed to view the body. Low cries could be heard throughout the room mixed in with Marvin Sapp's "Here I am" as it played over the sound system. Madysen's knees buckled as she watched the pictures of Max glide across the screen ahead. Both brothers tightened their arms around her to hold her up.

"Take her through this row and sit down with her up front. As a matter of fact, we will all beat the crowd and wait until it clears to go up," Beast instructed them.

We all cut through the row and went to the front of the chapel to sit in the family section. Madysen got a glimpse of Max's body when a group of people moved past the casket and freaked out. It took all of us to calm her down. I wanted to take her out to get some air but she didn't want to leave. She was taking seeing him lying there very hard.

The music changed and Tamela Mann's "Take Me to the King" started playing. The line was getting longer and it was almost time for the funeral to start. Beast got up and said something to the pastor and he shook his head up and down.

Beast came back and sat next to me, "what's going on?" I asked.

"I explained that we didn't get a chance to view the body and he said we would get the opportunity before they closed the casket for the service."

Ricio's eyes were trained on Max and tears were rolling down his face. He put his hands on the top of his head and his shoulders shook with every tear that fell. Nija got up and went to his side and rubbed his back with her head on his shoulder.

Ten minutes later, the pastor walked up to us, letting us know we could view the body. Ricio and Nija led the pack and we all crowded around looking down at Max's lifeless body. My baby looked like he was sleeping. He was wearing the hell out of the white suite I bought for him and his fedora was resting on his chest. His casket matched the colors that we wore with a white lining. Inside the lid were the words, 'I'm going home.'

Nija forced Ricio to be strong when she started crying uncontrollably at the casket. Madysen didn't make things better when she damn near climbed inside with Max. Beast and Sosa had to pick her up and carry her away so they could close the casket. As they lowered the lid, Madysen screamed, "He won't be able to breathe! Please don't close him in there!"

Beast was trying to console her but she wouldn't let him. I sat next to her and wrapped her in my arms. She went limp and all I could do was fan her to keep her cool. Nija had a bottled water in her purse and I wet a few napkins, wiping her face. She opened her eyes after a while but continued to cry.

The pastor started the funeral. "This is one funeral that I didn't think I would be doing. I've known this young man since he came out his mother's womb. He had everything going for himself. I officiated his father's funeral four years ago, and three months later I did the same for his mother. Now here it is today, I'm doing it again for Maximo. Max as he was called, was a bright kid. For him to get caught up in the gunplay that has taken over this city, hurts my heart. I want all you young people to put the guns down! Life is short, make the best of it while you can. This young man didn't think his life would end at the tender age of eighteen, *eighteen*! He was still trying to figure out what he wanted to do with his life. I'm seeing this too often nowadays, it's not the way to go. No parent or loved one is prepared to bury a child. Live your life right starting today. To the family, Max wouldn't want y'all to cry for him. Let's read John 14:1 *'Do not let your hearts be troubled. You believe in God. Believe also in me.'* Believe that Max is alright, living in a more peaceful place than where we are. Max is reunited with both his parents, and now it's his job to watch over all of you. Hold on to each other, make sure everyone gets through this together."

When the pastor finished his Eulogy, then the choir stood and started singing 'Precious Lord' by Mahalia Jackson and there wasn't a dry eye in the house. As strong as I was trying to be, I couldn't hold back the tears that I fought hard not to let escape my eyes. After the song ended, the obituary was read silently. We opted not to have the casket opened again at the end of the service because we just didn't want to put ourselves through that again.

We had many volunteers that took flowers out to the hearse and Beast, Ricio, Sosa, Psycho, Felon, AK, Fats, and Alejandro carried Max's casket out of the building. Nija and I led Madysen to the car so we could line up to go to the cemetery. After I pulled the car to the front, I saw Beast standing talking to Chuck. I walked briskly over to them.

"Yeah, I didn't like what Big Jim said to me at the prison the day Max's funeral was announced on the news. I went to the security room and went back to the day Max came to visit and what I found, you are not going to like. I erased all evidence from the hard drive after I made a copy. Look at this footage, fam. That nigga is foul. The questions that y'all have, will be answered when you look at that, I promise. I'm gon' get out of here. I just wanted to come pay my respects, and give you that disc. Oh yeah, Big Jim is pissed off about what Rodrigo did to his boy Red. They are planning to attack some time today. Keep yo' eyes open," Chuck said before he blended in with the crowd and disappeared.

"What's on the disc, bae?" I asked with concern.

"I won't know until I get home. We will find out together before I take it to Ricio and Sosa," Beast said as he put the disc in the inside pocket of his jacket.

Waiting for all the cars to line up for the possession to the cemetery. The Vasquez boys came over to let us know nothing was out of the norm. It was good to hear that but I knew it was going to be short lived. Ricio and Nija was talking off to the side and Kimmie was chatting with Sosa

Renegade Boys

when Rod stepped out of the funeral home. I was shocked that he had the nerve to come to the funeral.

"What the hell is he doing here?" I asked Beast.

"Who?" he asked looking around. When he spotted Rodney, so did Ricio. They both headed in Rodney's direction but Psycho got to him first. Beast pulled Ricio back and said, "Let him take care of his business."

Whatever Psycho said to his father, made him get in his car and drive off. Ricio didn't like the fact that Rodney drove away without a scratch on his body. He approached Psycho and got in his face.

"Why didn't you handle that shit?" Ricio asked angrily.

"You wanted me to kill him in front of everybody out here, Ricio? I told him I would be by later tonight and he better be there. It will get handled tonight."

"It better or else. I'm about to bury my brother behind them muthafuckas. He's gon' pay," Ricio said jumping in his car.

The hearse was getting ready to pull off and it was time to head to the cemetery. There was a long line of cars trailing the hearse. It was an easy ride. There weren't any incidents along the way. We pulled into the gates of Lincoln Cemetery thirty minutes later.

Max was being buried next to Reese and Maritza. When Reese died, we bought five plots so their family would be together again in death. Ricio and the guys carried Max's casket to the burial site and placed the casket down. The pastor said a prayer and we let go eighteen doves in honor of the eighteen years Max lived on this earth.

After the casket was lowered into the ground, the crowd started dispersing to their cars. Sosa was kneeling on the side of the hole when gunshots erupted out of nowhere.

207

People were scrambling for cover to avoid getting hit. I pushed Madysen behind a tree and snatched out both of my guns.

I saw the infamous black Impala come to a halt. I fired at the car and it backed up rolling over graves. Three more vehicles sped up with gunfire flying from the windows. Sosa jumped up with gun in hand, busting at the cars that had muthafuckas hanging out the windows with blue bandanas on their faces.

Taking aim, we all were shooting at all the cars without giving them a chance to get anymore shots off. A couple of people got shot in the process but we were all still standing shooting like we were at war in Afghanistan. I had a clear view of someone in the black Impala at and I let my tool rock.

BOC BOC BOC BOC

I hit the person that was hanging out the back window four times in the chest, sending his ass flying back inside. A few more of their men got hit and they were retreating out of the cemetery. I ran toward the cars and someone fired three shots. Two of them hit me square in the chest while the other whizzed past my head barely missing me.

"Sin!" I heard Beast scream my name but it seemed so far away. It sounded like my name was being called in slow motion. My chest felt like it was on fire, then everything went black as I struggled to take a breath.

To Be Continued...

Submission Guideline

Submit the first three chapters of your completed manuscript to ldpsubmissions@gmail.com, subject line: Your book's title. The manuscript must be in a .doc file and sent as an attachment. Document should be in Times New Roman, double spaced and in size 12 font. Also, provide your synopsis and full contact information. If sending multiple submissions, they must each be in a separate email.

Have a story but no way to send it electronically? You can still submit to LDP/Ca$h Presents. Send in the first three chapters, written or typed, of your completed manuscript to:

**LDP: Submissions Dept
Po Box 870494
Mesquite, Tx 75187**

DO NOT send original manuscript. Must be a duplicate.

Provide your synopsis and a cover letter containing your full contact information.

Thanks for considering LDP and Ca$h Presents.

<u>Coming Soon from Lock Down Publications/Ca$h Presents</u>

BOW DOWN TO MY GANGSTA

By **Ca$h**

TORN BETWEEN TWO

By **Coffee**

BLOOD STAINS OF A SHOTTA **III**

By **Jamaica**

STEADY MOBBIN **III**

By **Marcellus Allen**

BLOOD OF A BOSS **V**

By **Askari**

LOYAL TO THE GAME **IV**

LIFE OF SIN

By **T.J. & Jelissa**

A DOPEBOY'S PRAYER **II**

By **Eddie "Wolf" Lee**

IF LOVING YOU IS WRONG… **III**

LOVE ME EVEN WHEN IT HURTS **II**

By **Jelissa**

TRUE SAVAGE **VI**

By **Chris Green**

BLAST FOR ME **III**

A BRONX TALE

By **Ghost**

ADDICTIED TO THE DRAMA **III**

By **Jamila Mathis**

LIPSTICK KILLAH **III**

CRIME OF PASSION **II**

By **Mimi**

WHAT BAD BITCHES DO **III**

KILL ZONE **II**

By **Aryanna**

THE COST OF LOYALTY **II**

By **Kweli**

SHE FELL IN LOVE WITH A REAL ONE **II**

By **Tamara Butler**

LOVE SHOULDN'T HURT **III**

RENEGADE BOYS **II**

By **Meesha**

CORRUPTED BY A GANGSTA **IV**

By **Destiny Skai**

A GANGSTER'S CODE **III**

By **J-Blunt**

KING OF NEW YORK III

By **T.J. Edwards**

CUM FOR ME **IV**

By **Ca$h & Company**

GORILLAS IN THE BAY

De'Kari

THE STREETS ARE CALLING

Duquie Wilson

KINGPIN KILLAZ II

Hood Rich

STEADY MOBBIN' **III**

Marcellus Allen

SINS OF A HUSTLA II

ASAD

HER MAN, MINE'S TOO **II**

Nicole Goosby

GORILLAZ IN THE BAY **II**

DE'KARI

TRIGGADALE II

Elijah R. Freeman

THE STREETS ARE CALLING **II**

Duquie Wilson

Available Now

RESTRAINING ORDER **I & II**

By **CA$H & Coffee**

LOVE KNOWS NO BOUNDARIES **I II & III**

By **Coffee**

RAISED AS A GOON I, II, III & IV

BRED BY THE SLUMS I, II, III

BLAST FOR ME I & II

ROTTEN TO THE CORE I III

By **Ghost**

LAY IT DOWN **I & II**

LAST OF A DYING BREED

BLOOD STAINS OF A SHOTTA I & II

By **Jamaica**

By **TJ & Jelissa**

By **T.J. Edwards**

By **Jelissa**

By **Jibril Williams**

By **Meesha**

By **J-Blunt**

By **Bre' Hayes**

By **Askari**

By **Jerry Jackson**

CUM FOR ME

CUM FOR ME 2

CUM FOR ME 3

An **LDP Erotica Collaboration**

BRIDE OF A HUSTLA **I II & II**

THE FETTI GIRLS **I, II& III**

CORRUPTED BY A GANGSTA I, II & III

By **Destiny Skai**

WHEN A GOOD GIRL GOES BAD

By **Adrienne**

A GANGSTER'S REVENGE **I II III & IV**

THE BOSS MAN'S DAUGHTERS

THE BOSS MAN'S DAUGHTERS II

THE BOSSMAN'S DAUGHTERS III

THE BOSSMAN'S DAUGHTERS IV

THE BOSS MAN'S DAUGHTERS **V**

A SAVAGE LOVE **I & II**

BAE BELONGS TO ME

A HUSTLER'S DECEIT I, II

WHAT BAD BITCHES DO I, II

By **Aryanna**

A KINGPIN'S AMBITON

A KINGPIN'S AMBITION **II**

I MURDER FOR THE DOUGH

By **Ambitious**

TRUE SAVAGE

TRUE SAVAGE II

TRUE SAVAGE **III**

TRUE SAVAGE **IV**

TRUE SAVAGE **V**

By **Chris Green**

A DOPEBOY'S PRAYER

By **Eddie "Wolf" Lee**

THE KING CARTEL **I, II & III**

By **Frank Gresham**

THESE NIGGAS AIN'T LOYAL **I, II & III**

By **Nikki Tee**

GANGSTA SHYT **I II &III**

By **CATO**

THE ULTIMATE BETRAYAL

By **Phoenix**

BOSS'N UP **I , II & III**

By **Royal Nicole**

I LOVE YOU TO DEATH

By Destiny J

I RIDE FOR MY HITTA

I STILL RIDE FOR MY HITTA

By **Misty Holt**

LOVE & CHASIN' PAPER

By **Qay Crockett**

TO DIE IN VAIN

By **ASAD**

BROOKLYN HUSTLAZ

By **Boogsy Morina**

BROOKLYN ON LOCK I & II

By **Sonovia**

GANGSTA CITY

By **Teddy Duke**

A DRUG KING AND HIS DIAMOND I & II III

A DOPEMAN'S RICHES

HER MAN, MINE'S TOO

By Nicole Goosby

TRAPHOUSE KING **I II & III**

KINGPIN KILLAZ

By **Hood Rich**

LIPSTICK KILLAH **I, II**

CRIME OF PASSION

By **Mimi**

STEADY MOBBN' **I, II**

By **Marcellus Allen**

WHO SHOT YA **I, II**

Renta

GORILLAZ IN THE BAY

DE'KARI

TRIGGADALE

Elijah R. Freeman

GOD BLESS THE TRAPPERS I, II, III

THESE SCANDALOUS STREETS I, II, III

FEAR MY GANGSTA I, II

THESE STREETS DON'T LOVE NOBODY I, II

Tranay Adams

BOOKS BY LDP'S CEO, CA$H

TRUST IN NO MAN

TRUST IN NO MAN 2

TRUST IN NO MAN 3

BONDED BY BLOOD

SHORTY GOT A THUG

THUGS CRY

THUGS CRY 2

THUGS CRY 3

TRUST NO BITCH

TRUST NO BITCH 2

TRUST NO BITCH 3

TIL MY CASKET DROPS

RESTRAINING ORDER

RESTRAINING ORDER 2

IN LOVE WITH A CONVICT

Coming Soon

BONDED BY BLOOD 2

BOW DOWN TO MY GANGSTA

Renegade Boys